Simon Eichel

The Patriarch. Two Stories of Jewish Life

Ulrich Frank

Alpha Editions

This edition published in 2023

ISBN : 9789357930451

Design and Setting By
Alpha Editions
www.alphaedis.com
Email - info@alphaedis.com

SIMON EICHELKATZ

To-day I was called to attend an old man who lives at the Flour Market, almost opposite the "New" Synagogue. The messenger told me I could not possibly miss the house, because the steps leading up to the old man's rooms were built on the outside; and this is in peculiar contrast to the modern architecture prevailing in the city. In fact, I do not know whether another house so curiously constructed is to be seen anywhere else in the place. And so I found it without much questioning. At any rate, I knew of the New Synagogue. I have never entered it, yet a soft, secret wave of religious feeling creeps over me each time I pass it, and that happens frequently. The synagogue lies on the road to the extensive factory quarter built up by one of the large manufacturers for his employees. My professional duties often take me there.

The synagogue!—I always look at the simple structure, devoid of ornament, with mixed feelings of veneration and awe. I hold tradition in high regard. After all it counts for something that a man is the offspring of a pious race, which cherishes learning and *Yichus*. How does the Hebrew word happen to come to me? The synagogue keeps its grip on what belongs to it—and on me, too! Yet I should not be able to pray within its walls— although it was in such a place as this synagogue that my father taught the word of God.

In fact, is it possible for us moderns still to pray? And then those remarkable Hebrew words, unintelligible to most of us now—*Ovinu Malkenu!* The Church has converted them into the Lord's Prayer, the most fervent of its prayers. *Ovinu Malkenu!* I see myself a little chap standing next to my father. How surcharged these words with belief and faith and hope when spoken by him: *Ovinu Malkenu chosvenu be-Sefer Parnossoh ve-Chalkoloh*— "Give us this day our daily bread!"

Synagogue and church! Hebrew or German or Latin? The shrill call of the Shofar, or the soft sense-enslaving tones of the organ? I believe modern man can pray only in the dumb speech of the heart.

It seems to me, if I were all alone in a synagogue, a devout mood would come over me; I would pray there. In Florence this happened to me once. It was very early in the morning; I was alone in a small church on the other side of the Arno, Santa Maria del Carmine, whose frescoes, painted by Masaccio, declare the joy and jubilation of man over his beauty and greatness. But, I remember, the words were Hebrew that sprang up in my heart, even if they did not pass my lips. So the dumb language of the soul has its familiar tones, its words endeared by association.

Truth compels me to admit that it was Simon Eichelkatz who prompted me to put these thoughts of mine down in writing.

My patient at the Flour Market! When I climbed the steep stairway, thoroughly scoured and strewn with white sand, I little suspected I should soon stand in the presence of one of the most interesting persons it had ever been my good fortune to meet. The stairway led directly into the kitchen. A long, lank individual received me there, and on my asking for Herr Eichelkatz, he answered testily: "I guess he's in the floored room." At the moment I could not imagine what he meant. Then I noticed that the flooring of the kitchen was only of cement, and I realized that he meant to convey that the room in which the patient waited had a wooden flooring.

"Will you lead me there?" I asked politely.

"Lead!" with a deprecating shrug of the shoulders. "Why should I lead? It's right here. They must be led. These new-fashioned people must be led. Can't they walk by themselves?" At these not very friendly words, he pushed a door open and bawled in: "The doctor is here—the Herr Kreisphysikus. I should lead him to you, Reb Shimme. By himself he would never find you. Reb Shimme, should I drive him in with the white or the black horse? It's too far for him, Reb Shimme, the new-fashioned people want to be led; they want to be announced by a vally. Whether they come to a king or to Reb Shimme Eichelkatz, it's all the same, they must be announced."

All this was accompanied by scornful chuckles; and he looked at me angrily, quite taken aback, when I pushed him aside with a sweep of my arm just as he cried out again: "Herr Kenig, the doctor is here!"

I stood in the middle of the room, the "floored" room, and, verily, I stood in the presence of a kingly man, I stood before Simon Eichelkatz.

SEPTEMBER 16.

What is it that draws me to this old man? I am almost glad he needs my care as a physician. Remarkable egotism this on my part; but fortunately the sickness is not serious; a slight indisposition, such as often comes in old age. My patient is well on in the seventies, and is really wonderfully fresh and vigorous. A sudden spell of faintness induced his servant to send for me—the wrathful, snarling servant who received me with so little grace on my first visit. Now I am used to Feiwel Silbermann's quirks and sallies. I know his intentions are not bad; and then his great merit in my eyes is his rare fidelity to Simon Eichelkatz. After I had finished examining the patient on my first visit, Feiwel crept after me, caught hold of me as I stood on the lowest step, and anxiously inquired:

"What is the matter with Reb Shimme? Is he, God forbid, really sick? He's never been this way before. I've known him—may he long be spared—these twenty years, but as he was to-day—"

Feiwel tried to take my hand. "I must scold, *nebbich*. That's what he's used to. And if I were suddenly to come along with fine manners, he might think, *Chas ve-Sholem*, it was all over with him. Now, I ask you, Herr Kreisphysikusleben, if a man always scolds and means well, isn't that as good as if a man speaks softly and is false? A treacherous dog doesn't bark. Praised be God, Reb Shimme knows what he's got in me. Twenty years I've been with him, since Madame Eichelkatz died. His only son is professor at the University in Berlin. A *Meshummed*, Herr Doktor. Baptized," he added, his voice growing hoarse. "Since the gracious Madame Eichelkatz died, we live here, at the Flour Market. And he never saw his son again, Herr Doktor. But now, if he should, God forbid, get sick—he's an old man—I don't know what I should do."

Ah! So Simon Eichelkatz has a skeleton in his closet, not an every-day skeleton, either. I should not have suspected it from what I saw of the gentle, gay-spirited old man. As to Feiwel, I set his worries at rest. I told him the illness was not serious, a mere weakness, not unusual in a man of Simon Eichelkatz's age, and it would pass without serious consequences. Feiwel gave me a look of such devout gratitude that I was touched. "Of course," I said, "you must be watchful, and must take good care of him, because at his age every symptom must be taken into account."

"What, symtohn he has?" Feiwel asked, anxious again. "Can symtohn become dangerous? Is it a very bad trouble? Symtohn!" He repeated the word several times. "I've heard of people's getting heart disease, or kidney trouble, may I be forgiven for my sins, or rheumatiz, but to get symtohn!"

I explained the meaning of the word to him, and he breathed a sigh of relief.

"Praised be God, if it's nothing more than that—I'll look out for the symtohns, you can be sure of that, Herr Kreisphysikusleben."

"I'll come again to-morrow to find out how Herr Eichelkatz is doing," I said, "and I hope it won't be necessary to let Herr Professor Eichelkatz know—"

At that moment it occurred to me I had never heard of a university professor of that name.

"He isn't called Eichelkatz at all," Feiwel whispered with spite in his voice. "If a man can have himself baptized, he can throw his father's name away, too. Why not? What should a man be named Eichelkatz for if he's a professor? If he's a professor, it's better for him *evadde* to be named Eichner—such a name!"

Eichner! Professor Friedrich Eichner, the most powerful of modern thinkers, the philosopher of world-wide renown, a son of Simon Eichelkatz!

SEPTEMBER 22.

I see the New Synagogue now every day. It was dedicated over forty years ago, but it is still called "New." They had a rabbi come from Berlin to dedicate it, and that after their own rabbi had worked for ten long years to make the building possible, after he had gone to great pains to scrape the money together, after his ardent appeals had succeeded in warming his people up to the undertaking, after he had removed all the difficulties presented by the authorities—after he had brought things so far, his congregation found it in their hearts to humiliate him at the crowning point of his achievement, they found it in their hearts to set him aside at the dedication in favor of another.

Have honor and justice come back to you? Have the years left their traces upon you, O ye, whom I love, my brethren in faith? Forty years! New generations have blossomed since those days when pride and false ambition brought sorrow to a noble spirit, and sought to deprive him of the fruits of his labor, blessed and pleasing to the Lord. Another was permitted to take his place and consecrate the work he had called into being. On the day of his greatest glory they poured gall into his soul, filled his heart with bitterness. But he forgave!

Gradually I am learning all sorts of stories about the congregation. Simon Eichelkatz tells them to me when I visit him, and that happens almost daily. It is now one of my favorite recreations to hunt up this old man, this wise old man; for what he says in that easy, simple way of his always awakens new thoughts in me. He little suspects the abundance, the wealth of ideas that arise and take form in his mind. They all well forth so unconsciously, the most profound and the most exalted. One day a granite rock of Kantian philosophy towers up before me; the next day the trumpet tones of a Nietzsche reveille sound in my ears. And this feeble old man, who gives utterance to these deep thoughts, never read any other book than the book of life, life in a small town remote from the bustle of the world, life in a Jewish community, with its intellectual backwardness and provincial peculiarities. The *Khille*, it is true, with its concentric circles, its conservatism, its solidarity, its self-sufficiency, was rich soil to foster individuality and develop reserve strength. Nothing is wasted there, nothing consumed too quickly in those communities thrown back upon themselves, leading, forced to lead, a life apart from the rest of the world. How much that is of import to the world has gone forth from such communities! When the seed had grown strong and healthy in its native soil, and was then transplanted to fresh soil, how it blossomed forth, fruit-bearing, fructifying!

Now it seems to me as though Professor Friedrich Eichner could not possibly have been of other parentage. The son, the heir of Simon Eichelkatz! With amazement, with rapture we listened to his lectures, to which students from all the other departments also crowded; and when the world-philosophies he unfolded loomed before our eyes in gigantic proportions, a feeling came over us of shuddering awe and admiration. Who was this man? A radical, an iconoclast. And now, out of the mouth of an old man, I hear ideas, conceptions, truths that might have laid the foundations for the philosophy of the other, the younger, man. Not that the relation between them was that of teacher and pupil; for Professor Friedrich Eichner knew nothing of his father's wisdom, and the father knew nothing of his son's philosophic systems. The father does not mention his son—he probably is ignorant of his son's life, of his son's importance to science. Only once he referred to him, recently, in telling me about the "New" Synagogue. Sunk in thought he said:

"The first *Bar-Mitzvah* that took place there was my son's. I still remember the speech our *Rav* delivered then—about the love of parents and fidelity to those who lead us in our youth—Herr Kreisphysikus, our Rav was a fine, sensible man, but he did not understand just what a child should be. The child should grow away from us, above us, larger, stronger, and higher—and we mustn't ask anything of him, and we mustn't say to him, 'Come and stay here with me, where it is cramped and stuffy for want of air—enough air for an old man, but too little for you. And you shall not be my child, not a child, a filly, that neighs for the stable where its father and mother roll on the straw like animals. You must keep on growing—you must be a man, not a child.'"

Simon Eichelkatz—Friedrich Eichner!

My heart is tender, and I love my dear mother, whom a kindly fate has preserved for me unto this day; and I bless and honor the memory of my dead father. My opinion about filial and parental relations is entirely different from Simon Eichelkatz's; but it seemed to me as though I were listening to a chapter of Nietzsche's Zarathustra. Never did this name sound in your ears, Simon Eichelkatz. You never left the Khille, and for twenty years you have been living alone with your bodyguard, Feiwel

Silbermann. But your son has written great works concerning the Zarathustra doctrine.

SEPTEMBER 24.

The members of the Jewish community here are beginning to look upon me as a queer sort of person. In a measure, it is the duty of a new physician of the Jewish belief to associate with the "gentry" among his co-religionists. That is what is expected of me; and certainly I ought long ago to have left my card at the doors of the Jewish families that are well-to-do, and, as they think, aristocratic and cultivated. On my desk lies a long, imposing list of persons of consequence, and it is my firm intention to pay them my respects; my predecessor urgently recommended me to do so. "You will get into things most quickly," he said, "if you make your way among the well-to-do Jewish families. The community has a reputation from of old for setting great store by culture and refinement; and what better for you in a small out-of-the-way place than a stimulus now and then in the form of a visit to some pleasant home? The evenings are long; you can't forever be playing Skat." I certainly can't, because I know precious little about the game—and so the cultivated Jewish families are my future here. For the present I have found something else, which gives me more than I can expect from the stimulus of would-be æsthetic Jewish wives and maidens.

I dearly love my fellow-Jews. But my love for them must not blind me to their weaknesses, and among their weaknesses I count an assumption of culture, a pseudo-refinement of the intellect, which has taken increasing hold upon the daughters of our race. How often I was disagreeably impressed by them in Berlin when they spoke about anything and everything, with that half-culture which produces the feeling that they are not concerned with knowledge, but with the effect to be created by their apparent "information" upon all subjects. What don't they know! What don't they want to know! How often I was tempted to say to one or another of them: "The learning of many things does not cultivate the mind; learn to believe and to think." And must I repeat the same experience here? I am uneasy; my predecessor sentimentalized too much about the "educated" Jewesses. Some of them, he unluckily told me, had been "finished off" in prominent educational institutions in foreign countries. I know all that, and I'm afraid of it, this finishing-off process of the ladies' seminaries! But probably there will be nothing else for me to do. If the winter evenings here are really so long and dreary, I may not be able to resist the torment of hearing young lips, soft and rosy for kissing, put the question to me: "What do you think of Nietzsche's 'Beyond evil and good,'" or "Do you think the painters of the Quatrocento and the Secessionists have anything in common?" How that hurts! Almost a physical pain! At all events it has often spoilt my taste for kissing soft, rosy lips.

If I would seek wisdom, if I would drink at the source of life, here, in this place, I shall not go to youth, but to old age.

I spent some time again with Simon Eichelkatz this afternoon. Outside it was raining and storming. A raw, grey day of autumn, the first this year. Up to this time the weather has been good. Over the small, quiet room a something brooded, something contemplative, genial, spiritual. Half dream-like, half meditative. Like the dying away of a great melody. I wondered if Simon Eichelkatz had ever heard of *Stimmungen*. I longed to put the question to him. "Tell me, Reb Shimme" (that is how I call him now), "when you are here all by yourself, in this great silence, do you ever have a feeling as if—as if—how should I say?—as if you were a part of your surroundings, as if everything that is about you helped along to give form to certain ideas in your mind?"

I had to smile as I put the question. "Now say *milieu*," I scoffed at myself; and yet I never before felt the significance of the word so strongly as in that moment. The old man looked at me as though he wanted to find the meaning of the incomprehensible question in my face. His gaze, still clear and keen, rested on me thoughtfully, then passed quickly through the room, as though this would bring him enlightenment upon the relevancy of my question. Finally, he said slowly, as though he were formulating his thoughts only with difficulty:

"I hear the silence about me—is that what you mean, Herr Doktor? I hear the silence, and so I am not alone. My soul is not deaf, and everything about me speaks to me. And the table has a language, and the chair on which I sit, and my pipe, Herr Doktor, my long pipe, it talks a good deal—and the *Kiddush* cup here, and the spice-box—I wonder what they have lived through and have to tell about—and when the sun shines outside and peeps through the window, it's one thing, and when it rains like to-day, it's another." He rested his head on his hand. "But the silence is never dead—it lives as I live."

Friedrich Eichner's form rose before me, as it looked several years ago, when I heard him in his lecture room speak on Zarathustra's "still hour."

"That's just what is called *Stimmungen*, Reb Shimme," I said, as in a confused dream. He nodded his head several times, but said nothing in response.

SEPTEMBER 25.

To-day Simon Eichelkatz told me about Rabbi Dr. Merzbach. This is his favorite topic. He finds the most forceful expressions when he gets to talking about him. "That was a man!" he exclaims over and over again, "fine, clever, good—much too good for the *Parchonim* in the Khille. My, how it did look when he came here! I remember it as though it were yesterday. The first *Shabbes* in *Shul*—it was still the old Shul—they little dreamed a time would come when there would be a 'New Synagogue.' And *he* built it. The old one was almost more below the ground than above it. And that's the way the people here were, too. Black! Black of heart, black of morals! And first he built a new synagogue in the spirits of the people, and then he built a synagogue of stone and wood, so that they could hold their services in a worthy place. That's what he said, Herr Doktor, I can hear him preaching yet; and I learned much from what he said, for I never missed a sermon, and, besides, he was good and friendly toward me and spoke with me as often as he saw me. A great scholar—a real Doktor, not just a *Talmid Chochom*; he knew other things, too. On that first Shabbes, the old Shul was so full that the people stood out on the street, and they were so quiet, you could hear every word. And there he preached, like Mosheh Rabbenu when he came down from Mount Sinai to the Children of Israel. Not that they were bad, he told them, but that they must become better. And that they must not let themselves be ruled by their instincts and desires, but that each one must work away at himself to become nobler, more intelligent, and that each one could do this, because it was his Divine heritage, which was given to every man when God created him in His image. And they should be proud to be men, and for that they should acquire the dignity of man. It sounded glorious; and even if they didn't understand him, they were so touched, they would cry, and say it was rare good fortune for the congregation that such a man had become their Rav. People came from all the places near here to listen to the sermons of Doktor Salomon Merzbach; and in the wine-room of Heimann at the Ring you heard about nothing else. Whoever was fine, or wanted to be considered fine, stuck to him at first, but still more the plain people and the poor and unfortunate, because to them he was like a messenger of God."

The narrator paused a while, as though he were letting the past take form again in his mind.

"He was gentle with the bad, and friendly and forbearing with the hardened and the malicious, and he explained to them, that if it was their will, they could be good, because the will was given to man to be exerted and to be conquered. I was still young then, and I did not understand him; but one thing I did understand, that a great and good man had come to preach in our wilderness."

Whence had Simon Eichelkatz taken these metaphors, these conceptions, these words? I stood before a great riddle.

"But later," he continued, "I understood what he meant. In ourselves there is nothing good and nothing bad; it is only what we do, how we act that determines the moral worth of things." I had to suppress an exclamation. I jumped up and hastily said good-night. It was positively uncanny to hear the new values, the basic principles of good and evil, conveyed by one so absolutely unsuspecting of their import. The Jews, without doubt, possess philosophic instincts.

When I stepped out into the open air, it was still raining. Impenetrable clouds hung low in the heavens, as if the whole world would sink down into the cold, trickling mass of fog. The steps leading down to the Flour Market were smooth and slippery. I groped my way cautiously.

"Verily, I say unto you: Good and evil that perishes not—there is no such thing. Out of itself it must always reconquer itself."

I said these words half aloud. I shivered, and worn and weary I crept home.

SEPTEMBER 26.

Now I know about how Dr. Salomon Merzbach looked. Simon Eichelkatz owns an old daguerreotype of him, which he cherishes carefully and honors as a holy relic. He showed it to me when I was there this morning. On the shining, mirror-like surface, the features were almost obliterated; but when I shaded it with my hand, they came out more distinctly. A fine, noble face, a lovable expression, and endlessly good. In the eyes a gleam as of hidden scorn, but benevolence, too, and good humor—perhaps some sadness. He looks, not as one who scoffs at the weaknesses of his fellow-men, but as one who pities them, sympathizes with them. The supernal humor of the wise man plays about the strong mouth with its somewhat sensuous lips. In studying the features, one feels the greatness and goodness of a pure nature. A narrow line of beard frames the face and rounds off under the strong chin, giving the countenance a clerical expression, reminding one more of a pastor than of a rabbi.

It was as though Simon Eichelkatz had guessed the tenor of my thoughts; for he suddenly said:

"What a fuss there was about the beard! The Orthodox raged, 'A Rav should wear a smooth face!' 'He looks as though he were shaved!' they screamed, although they knew perfectly well that a smooth skin can be gotten without a knife, with *aurum*—excuse me, Herr Kreisphysikus, aurum-stinkum is what we always called it when we were children. But the Orthodox wouldn't let on they knew anything about—stinkum! And how they did bother him on account of his beard and his tolerance! Right after his first great speech—I told you of it—they got together in the afternoon at *Sholosh Sudes*, at Reb Dovidel Kessler's, and began to agitate against him. 'What nonsense,' they screamed, 'there is no good and no evil! He's *meshugge!*

What sort of *Chochmes* is that? And he wears a new-fashioned beard, like a—priest, and a gown and a cap—and the *Talles* as narrow as a necktie—that wants to be a Rav.'"

That very day an opposition party was formed, which was against all the changes and necessary reforms Dr. Merzbach introduced. They worked in secret, like a mole underground, for no opposition dared show itself openly, because the richer and more intelligent in the congregation stuck to him. The young people especially were his faithful followers. On the Saturdays when he preached, the synagogue was always filled to overflowing. Besides, in the afternoon he got together in his house all who wanted to be enlightened on religious and moral questions; and they flocked to him like disciples to their master—to this man, who wanted to throw light upon the darkness of their ideas and notions. A nickname was soon coined for his opponents; they were called the "Saints." An underhand, double-tongued, cringing, vile lot they were in their libellous attacks upon Dr. Merzbach.

In telling me these things, even at this late day something like righteous indignation came over Simon Eichelkatz, usually so tranquil and unruffled.

"And all that the Khille owed him, too!" he exclaimed. "He improved our speech; through the power and beauty of his sermons he awakened in us the endeavor to cultivate a better, more refined language than the jargon we then spoke. Even now, when we get excited over what we're saying, it sometimes comes back to us. The younger generation had it easy; it glided right into the newer, better times. It was harder for us older men—we had little time for learning; but whoever wanted to understand him, he could—he could.

"I was already a married man when he came here. I had my business, and unfortunately I couldn't go to school any more; yet I did learn from him—to speak, Herr Kreisphysikus, and perhaps to think—though that came much later. Working and attending to business, you can't get to it. But I saw and heard everything the new rabbi undertook, and I followed it with interest, even though at that time I couldn't have a say in congregational affairs. And do you know what he did then? He started a school, a Jewish school, with nothing but trained teachers, the boys' school separate from the girls'. And you learned everything there, just as in the Christian schools. When he delivered the address at the opening of the school, he said that we were enjoying the blessings of the year 1848, which had brought us Jews the liberty, as citizens, to make use of all the privileges of culture and progress. And around him were the boys and girls dressed in their holiday clothes, and the parents full of gratitude. But the 'Saints' turned against him in these spiritual efforts, too, and the word 'progress' was like a red rag to a bull with them."

Simon Eichelkatz had a specially good day to-day. He related everything so vividly. It was as though the struggles of that time were still stirring in him. Naturally, the young business man, already the head of a household, placed himself entirely on the side of the liberals, who adhered to the rabbi, while the "others" spoke of the "new-fashioned" Rav with scorn and fanatical virulence, and made every attempt to overturn the institutions he had introduced.

"The changes he made in the service, above all a choir led by a cantor with musical training, also excited their anger. They came forward quite openly and arranged their own service under the leadership of Dovidel Kessler. But Rabbi Merzbach had consideration and pity for his enemies, and paid no attention to the way they threw mud at him. He was nothing less than a good, great man, and he would not let himself be hindered in his work. And for ten years of wicked struggles and bitter ill-will, he built his new synagogue in the hearts of his people, and at last the ground was prepared for it. Things became better, and, besides, he gave the people a common goal, the building of a new house of worship. Now they had an outlet for their energy—but an outlet, too, for their ambition and their vanity.

"That's the way it must be, Herr Kreisphysikus. The highest often comes forth from the lowest. And finally the synagogue stood there finished. What joy there was! And what a reward! But now I ask you, Herr Doktor, can't life be without the riff-raff? Is dirt a constituent of cleanliness?"

Again those remarkable observations!

"Are poisoned wells necessary, and evil-smelling fires, and foul dreams, and maggots in the bread of life?"

Comparisons from Zarathustra are always forcing themselves into my mind. Whence this wisdom, Simon Eichelkatz? And do you suspect there is an answer to these questions?

"Verily, we have no abiding-places prepared for the unclean. Unto their bodies our happiness would be an icy cave, and unto their spirits as well. Like strong winds we would live above them, neighbors to the eagles, neighbors to the snow, neighbors to the sun; thus do the strong winds live."

My eye fell again on the daguerreotype—were you a strong wind, Rabbi Dr. Merzbach? You blew away many a crumbling ruin of the past. Yet you knew naught of the new values. You did not know that you must call to your enemies, to them that spit at you: "Take heed that ye spit not in the face of the wind." You lived in the times of the daguerreotype.

I asked Simon Eichelkatz for permission to make a number of copies of the picture with my excellent photographic apparatus which I use for the Röntgen rays.

SEPTEMBER 28.

The *Rebbetzin*! The word brings a wealth of pictures before my mind. I see my good mother living quietly, modestly, in the little town in which my father of blessed memory was rabbi. When he died—it was just when I was taking the state examination—I wanted to persuade her to move with me to Berlin. She would not. "Here I am at home, here is the grave of my husband of blessed memory, here are the graves of my dear parents and of my brothers and sisters; here lie your two sisters, who died young—here is my world. Everybody knows me, and I know everybody. What should I do in Berlin among nothing but strangers? I would worry and never feel at ease, and I would only hinder you in your profession. Leave me where I am. Old trees should not be transplanted. And here I can live decently on what I have. In the big city, where living is high, it wouldn't hold out. If only you will write often to me, and visit me every year, I shall have a happy, blessed old age."

This is the arrangement I have kept up, and hope to keep up many more years. My dear little mother is well and robust; and in the modest corner she has fitted up for herself, dwell genuine peace and true humility. Humility! That is not exactly the characteristic mark of a Rebbetzin. The real Rebbetzin, the one who is exactly what a Rebbetzin should be, is proud and conscious of her dignity. The more modest and simple the Rav, the haughtier and more exigent the Rebbetzin.

"And that's altogether natural," said Simon Eichelkatz to me to-day. "The Jews like to lead the people they employ a dance, and they are hard-hearted and domineering toward the weak and the dependent."

This is an unexplained trait in the soul of the Jewish race. Possibly, it is due to the fact that they are often contentious and want the last word in an argument. And then comes a man, fine, tranquil, peace-loving, thoughtful, as were most of the rabbis, especially in those days, fifty years ago, and immediately the spirit of contradiction stirs in the people; and the more they love and respect their rabbi, the more they worry and pester him. Everything in which they themselves are lacking—Talmudic learning, knowledge and culture, goodness, modesty, and self-effacement, the utmost piety and self-sacrifice—all this they demand of him.

"In a way he was to take upon himself all the *Tzores* and wickedness and stupidity of the *Baale-Batim*," continued Simon Eichelkatz, "and the more aggressions they allowed themselves, the more virtue they expected of him.

- 12 -

A wonder! *Nu*, Dr. Merzbach held up his end, and really atoned for the sins of the 'black' Khille."

At that time conditions were probably similar to these in all places in which rabbis of modern culture and academic training began to carry light and truth to the minds of the Jews, who through the persecutions and oppressions under which they had so long languished had become distrustful, secretive, cowardly, and embittered. It was no slight task. And many a rabbi, weak and faint-hearted, wrecked himself in the attempt. In that case, it was a piece of good fortune if the Rebbetzin saw to it that her husband did not suffer all that was put upon him, if she stood shoulder to shoulder with him, protecting, guarding him, warding off what foolishness, ill-nature, and tyrannical whims hatched against him. Usually the relation was this: the Rav they loved but vexed, the Rebbetzin they hated but feared. A certain equilibrium was thus maintained.

"And our Rebbetzin, Frau Dr. Merzbach, *she* was their match!" cried Simon Eichelkatz. "She was proud, and she looked down on the members of the congregation almost disdainfully. They couldn't hold a candle to her so far as family and position went; for she was the daughter of one of the best and most prominent families; and the piety and learning of her father and grandfather were known in all Israel. How could anyone in the Khille compare with her in breeding and birth?"

Simon Eichelkatz went on to tell me how these tradesmen and business men seemed like vassals to her. That was how she had been used to see the members of the congregation approach her father in his house; and she knew that was how they had approached her grandfather, with the deepest respect and devotion. And so the free way in which the people dared meet her husband, this forwardness and familiarity, wounded her beyond measure. And fearless and self-confident as she was, she made no secret of her feelings. This gave rise to eternal jarring; and again and again the Rav tried to reconcile her to the situation. But though she revered her husband as a saint and loved him with the self-surrender and faithfulness of a Jewish wife, she would not abandon her ground. Perhaps just because she loved him. She unconsciously felt that one could not get around the "rabble" merely with benevolence and mildness; firmness and haughtiness were also necessary in dealing with them. It is not unlikely that Dr. Merzbach could not have fought the fight to the finish if it had not been for his courageous wife. Certain it is that she kept many a slight from him, many an ill-natured offense. They all took care to let her alone; and when Frau Dr. Merzbach walked along the Ring, many a one slunk off around the corner, because his conscience pricked him on account of some gossip, some intrigue, or some petty persecution—these were the weapons with which the "Saints" agitated against the noble man. With his beautiful nature, he was no match for them, but they trembled before the Rebbetzin.

"And believe me, Herr Kreisphysikus," Simon Eichelkatz commented, "she was right; nothing else was left for her to do. That was the only way to get the better of that lying pack of hypocrites. If they hadn't been afraid of her, they would have fought even harder against the man who wanted to bring them the blessings of a regulated, proper life. They prepared enough bitterness for him, and he would probably have gotten tired and discouraged, gone to pieces sometimes, if his life in his own home had not weighed in the balance against the lowness of the Khille.

"And that's where the Rebbetzin was remarkable. She was just as clever as she was proud; and even her hottest opponents—and not all of them were of the Orthodox; some of the 'gentry' were envious of her and fought her—well, even her hottest opponents admitted that she was intelligent, and knew how to tackle things, that she tried to acquire modern culture, and that she gathered the better elements in the congregation about her. And her house was gay and refined, people felt at home there. Nowhere did one pass one's time so well as at Dr. Merzbach's."

The rabbi's house on his Friday evenings became a centre for the cultivated people, the people who held high places in the intellectual world of the congregation and the city. Christians, too, entered the circle.

"You can imagine, Herr Doktor, what bad blood that made. But the Rebbetzin didn't concern herself about it, and nobody could get a hold on her, because no fault could be found with her piety. Many said she was more orthodox than the Rav. There was some truth in this. He, being a great Talmudist, might find some freer interpretation of the laws, he might open up new ways, while she stuck fast to what had been sacred to her in her grandfather's and her father's home. I remember how he once came to my office on a very hot day, and took his hat off, and wiped his forehead, and then sat there without anything on his head, when suddenly his wife appeared outside in the store. He snatched up his hat, smiling in an embarrassed way, and said: 'God forbid my wife should see me sitting here without my cap.'"

Such trivialities and externalities invested her with glamour. Besides, there was her great philanthropy and her public work. Not a charitable institution belonging to the city or the congregation but that she was at the head of it. And outwardly cold and reserved, always carrying herself with great dignity, she still would willingly sacrifice herself in a good cause.

"During the cholera epidemic," continued Simon Eichelkatz, "I saw her at sick-beds, and I know what a heart she had, for all her fine intellect. But the others came no nearer to her, because they judged her according to her understanding alone, and that often made her appear hard and cold. But she didn't bother about things of that sort. She did not even have the wish to come nearer to those people; they seemed rude and uncultivated to her, and she was not in sympathy with them. Dr. Merzbach sometimes tried to make her change her opinion, but that was the point on which she would not yield, perhaps she couldn't. This was probably the one dark cloud on their blessed union, and it was a union that lasted through forty-three years of perfect agreement, of the purest and highest joy, of the greatest contentment.

"The Rebbetzin felt at home only in her own house; to the Khille she always remained a stranger. And do you know, Herr Kreisphysikus, when I come to think about it, I believe the Rebbetzin is always a stranger in the congregation? She can't fit herself in."

I had to smile. I thought of my mother, who was so different. But, to be sure, times have changed, and manners with them. And then the narrow little community in which my father worked, among friendly, kindly men and women! The "Rebbetzin" is probably a phenomenon belonging to a past epoch.

September 30.

Autumn is now completely upon us. Raw, gloomy, chilly, with everlasting rains. The city is not beautiful in this garb, and I would certainly succumb to my tendency to melancholy, if I did not have my profession and—Simon Eichelkatz.

He speaks about every possible thing. Only when the talk takes a personal turn, touching upon incidents in his life, he becomes monosyllabic and reserved. Consequently, I really know very little about him. With the exception of the hints once thrown out by Feiwel Silbermann about his "baptized" son Friedrich Eichner, I have learned nothing about him. It goes against me to question a servant, but I feel sure something lurks behind the sharp, ironic manner in which Feiwel on every occasion says "the gracious Madame Eichelkatz." Clearly, Madame Eichelkatz did not suit his taste. And I learn nothing from the people, either. I have not yet left my card with "the first Jewish families" of the congregation, and so I have not yet established any connections. But I really want to very soon. At present I feel more at home among the dead members of this congregation, all of whom, I hope, Simon Eichelkatz will by and by bring to life for me.

This world that has sunk into the past stirs my imagination, and I take deep interest in the figures that glided through the narrow streets fifty years ago. What constituted incidents in this world, what occupied these men, how they lived, loved, and hated—all this has a certain historic charm for me, heightened on account of my racial bias.

Yesterday Simon Eichelkatz promised to tell me all sorts of things during the fall and winter. I wonder whether I shouldn't wait a little while before I present my visiting cards. When once you begin, there are invitations and social obligations from which you cannot withdraw—and then there would be an end to the long talks with Simon. And I must carefully consider whether I am likely to laugh so heartily in the "æsthetic *salons*" of the fine Jewish houses as I did yesterday, when Simon told me the story of Teacher Sandberg. Scarcely! The young ladies would undoubtedly find the affair "shocking." But I want to record it here, and I will call it "The Adventure of Teacher Sandberg."

It was on the hottest and longest of Jewish fast days, *Shivoh oser be-Tamuz*. The sun glared down pitilessly. Not a breath of air to freshen, to quicken the heavy atmosphere. The Khille began the "three weeks" with a full fast day, on which the faithful partook neither of meat nor drink. The male members of the congregation strictly observed the customs, although to be pious was especially hard on this day in midsummer, when daylight continues endlessly. The length of the fast has become a byword, and a very tall man is said "to be as long as Shivoh oser be-Tamuz." But neither heat nor length prevented the faithful from keeping the fast recalling the destruction of the sanctuary on Zion. And so the congregation made itself penitential; it fasted, prayed, perspired, groaned, and denied itself every refreshment. The people crawled into the shadow of the houses to escape the heat and the tormenting thirst it caused. In vain! The awful sultriness penetrated everywhere, and brooded over the streets and dwellings, over field and meadow. The fasting men endured it with a certain apathy—after all, they were used to it; it repeated itself every year, and no one could remember that Shivoh oser be-Tamuz had ever fallen on a cool day. It couldn't be otherwise—in midsummer, the season of ripening fruits, of the harvest. You just had to accept the situation, and, in addition to the tortures of hunger and thirst, suffer those of heat as well. But on Shivoh oser be-Tamuz in 1853 a great fright came to swell the list of agonies in the Khille at Reissnitz.

Toward noon the report spread that the teacher Sandberg was missing. He had been seen in Shul at the morning service, and from there he had gone home, but after that he could not be traced further. Two boys who had been playing "cat" that morning in the street, declared they had seen him in front of his house, and then had noticed him go around the corner along the street leading to the so-called "Behnisch" meadows. That was the last that could be found out about Teacher Sandberg.

According to Simon Eichelkatz's description, he was a most singular individual. Extremely tall, and thin as a broom-stick, with a peculiar gait, rather pushing and scraping himself along the ground than walking. Summer and winter he wore a black silk cloth about his neck, above which showed only a very narrow line of white. His head was usually inclined to the left side in talking, and his whole face was cast into shadow by his large, beaked nose, ugly beyond belief. This nose of his was the butt of his pupils, the alphabet class of the congregational school. Sometimes it was a cause of terror to them as well, especially to the new pupils, who always needed some time to grow accustomed to it. But that happened as soon as Teacher Sandberg looked at them with his good-humored eyes, often gleaming with gayety, which allayed the fright produced by the uglier organ. In fact, it was the eloquence of his eyes that made the teacher a general favorite. Everyone liked the odd fellow; and from many a shop and window, sympathetic glances followed his figure as, with hands in his trouser pockets, he slouched along to school. One can therefore imagine the amazement caused by the news of his disappearance. Inquiry was made for him in the houses of neighboring families, the synagogue yard was searched,—perhaps he had taken refuge there from the heat,—every nook and cranny of his house, including the shop and cellar, were carefully investigated, the absurdest surmises as to his whereabouts were set afloat. Was he in some saloon? Impossible, on this fast day! His wife cried and sobbed, his children bawled—her husband, their father—where was he? Gone! As if swallowed by an earthquake! Not a single clue as to where he had disappeared. Some of the people, his weeping wife at their head, went to the "Behnisch" meadows. But he was not there; nor had he been seen by the harvesters taking their midday rest on the fresh stacks of hay. And why should he be there, in the maddening heat of high noon, hungry and thirsty from his fast? The mystery remained unsolved and began to assume a more and more terrifying aspect. What had driven him from his room? Whither had he wandered? Soon the word "accident" was anxiously whispered from mouth to mouth. But what could the nature of the accident be? In awe-stricken tones they hinted at murder! Suicide! God forbid that such suppositions should reach the ears of the wife and children! Crowds gathered in the White Suburb. They looked up and down the Gass, they glanced at the windows of Teacher Sandberg's house; they questioned one another, they propounded all sorts of theories, they debated and took counsel—Teacher Sandberg remained in the land of the unknown.

All forgot hunger and thirst, no one remembered that he was mortifying his flesh. What signifies so slight a sacrifice as compared with the awful fate that had befallen Teacher Sandberg? Fear and pity crept over the spirits of the people. What had happened? All the inhabitants of the city joined in the hunt with the relatives and co-religionists of the lost man. The whole little world was up and doing, excited, amazed, searching—and still Teacher Sandberg remained in the land of the unknown.

At two in the afternoon the rumor had spread from the White Suburb to the Ring, and penetrated into the quiet study of the rabbi. He immediately hurried to Teacher Sandberg's home, accompanied by the president, Herr Manasse, and the chairman of the board, Herr Karfunkelstein. He was also joined by all the other men in the congregation, by many women and children; and all streamed to the place excited and terrified, to get news of Teacher Sandberg's fate. The crowd in front of the unfortunate man's house was now so great that even the highly respected police also repaired thither; now all the citizens had assembled, and they talked with bated breath of the "unheard-of case." The rabbi and the president went inside the house to get the details again from the wife. The crowd waited outside expectantly. The rays of the midday sun beat down mercilessly. But no one thought of heat, hunger, or thirst. Everyone was occupied with Teacher Sandberg alone.

"Sandberg had to choose exactly Shivoh oser be-Tamuz to get lost on," said little Freund, the dealer in smoked meats. "He himself is as long as Shivoh oser be-Tamuz, and he had to have a misfortune just on the fast day."

"Just as if you were to put a fur coat on in this heat," said another man.

"No jokes," warned a third; "it's a sad business."

At that moment a man pushed his way through the crowd, breathless, gasping, in the greatest excitement. He was carrying a bag in which something swayed back and forth. The people looked at him with horror on their faces, and made way for him, carefully avoiding contact with the sack.

"Do you think it can be Sandberg's head that he's dragging in the bag?" The little dealer in smoked meat put the question anxiously.

"You can't tell!" answered his neighbor.

The man with the sack stepped into the passage way of the house, and the universal gaze was fastened with terrified curiosity upon the entrance. Minutes of the greatest expectation! That shuddering sense of oppression which precedes some dreadful occurrence had taken hold of all present. Not a single remark was passed, no sound was heard; the next moment was awaited in sheer breathless tension. A heavy weight rested on their spirits, the atmosphere was leaden, as before a storm; and yet the blue of the heavens was undimmed, not a single cloud flecked the horizon, and the sun's rays flamed with the heat of midsummer. So it was from a clear sky that a thunderbolt was to strike the expectant throng, and now—the rabbi came out to the top of the steps leading from the passage-way down to the street, on each side of him one of the directors, and behind him, in the open doorway, the man with the bag, now hanging over his shoulder empty. From within came sounds of mourning, crying, and sobbing. Expectation had reached its height, and the voice of Dr. Merzbach rang out through absolute quiet, as he said with deep seriousness:

"Beloved congregation! It has pleased the Almighty Father to let a sad and awful event occur in our midst on this fast day. Our highly respected teacher, Sandberg, whom we all know and love, the guide and instructor of our children, has met with a misfortune, a fact no longer permitting of doubt, since this man, a miller's apprentice from the Garetzki mill, found a pair of boots near the dam, and a red woolen handkerchief, which Frau Sandberg recognizes as unmistakably belonging to her husband. The miller met some hay-makers and learned from them that search was being made in the city for a lost man, and he came here immediately with the articles he had found. There can no longer be doubt as to the terrible truth, and we must bear with resignation the severe stroke the Lord has sent down upon the unfortunate family, so rudely robbed of its support and protection, and upon the community at large. On a day of atonement and repentance God has inflicted so hard a trial upon us."

At these words the people began to lament and weep. "*Waigeschrieen!* God cares nothing for our repentance!" some exclaimed, while others hit their breasts and cried: "*Oshamnu, bogadnu....*"

With great difficulty the rabbi succeeded in allaying the excitement. "Be sensible; keep quiet; we must see if it isn't possible still to help the unfortunate man, or at least we must find his corpse."

The words had an uncanny ring. A dark shadow seemed to creep over the bright day, the brilliant sunshine.

"It will be necessary for us to divide into bands to examine the banks of the stream from the mill-dam as far as the large sluice gate at the miner's dam. The water is shallow because of the drought of the past days, so there is still hope that some trace of him may be discovered. It would be well to take along a few persons who know how to swim, and provide others with poles. Our president will also see to it that the police help us in our search, and he will ask Garetzki, the proprietor of the mill, to let the water at the dam run off."

These directions, thoughtfully and quietly given, did not fail of their effect. Search parties were formed on the instant by Herr Moritz Liepmann, and sent in various directions. As they went toward the river, the wit of the

Khille, Reb Shmul Eisner, even at that critical moment could not repress the remark: "The idea of making *Tashlich* on Shivoh oser be-Tamuz."

Many Christians in the city joined the expedition, and the people sallied forth in the parching heat to hunt for Teacher Sandberg. The rabbi and the two trustees accompanied the crowd as far as the meadows bordering on the stream, and here a small posse branched off to go along the mill-race, to carry on the search along the tributary stream as well. Then Dr. Merzbach and his companions went to the meeting-room of the congregation in order to receive word there of the results of the investigation. Up and down the river went the people looking for Teacher Sandberg in the shallow spots. In vain! With the exception of a few irregular foot-prints in the moist soil near the mill-dam, nothing of note was discovered. Even the foot-prints were not of much significance, since they disappeared a short distance beyond the slope. Teacher Sandberg had completely disappeared. But one supposition was possible, that he had met with an accident. Probably in the glowing heat he had used the handkerchief to wipe away the perspiration, and had taken off his boots to cool his feet in the water, and in doing so had stepped into a deep spot, or overcome in the water by the heat, he had fainted, and drowned. A hundred guesses were made. But what remained the least explicable part of the mystery was why the teacher had gone out at all in the heat of high noon. In the meantime the day wore on. Hour after hour passed by. The searchers returned home dead-tired, hungry, and thirsty. In their zeal they had forgotten they were fasting; but at last the needs of the body asserted themselves. One by one they returned to the city. Each brought back the report of their vain endeavors; and when the last came back shortly before sunset, everybody was sure that Teacher Sandberg was no longer among the living. The rabbi once more went to Frau Sandberg to speak words of comfort to her and her children, and then the fateful day neared its end. There was scarcely a *Minyan* present at the evening services in the Shul. Pretty nearly every one remained at home with his family, doubly alive to the blessing of life in the face of this enigmatic death, and relishing the breaking of the fast with heightened appetite. For not a soul had lived through a fast day such as this before. When late in the evening the full moon hung above the houses, casting its white light on the open square and the streets, and the evening coolness had freshened the sultry air of the day, the people's spirits were re-animated, and they came out of their narrow dwellings into the open. All thronged to the Ring, the market place.

They felt the need of talking over the day's event. Before their doors sat the fathers of families, on green-painted benches, smoking their pipes, and discussing all the circumstances of the case. The women collected in groups, sympathizing with Frau Sandberg and breaking their heads over the problem as to what she would do, nebbich, now she was robbed of her supporter. The young people promenaded up and down, chatted in an undertone, and tried to be serious, in accord with the gravity of the situation, though they did not always succeed in banishing their youthful spirits. On the corner of Tarnowitzer Street stood Reb Shmul Eisner, the wit of the congregation. Half aloud he said to his neighbor: "Everybody is certainly happy not to be so famous as Teacher Sandberg is to-day."

The rabbi also came to the Ring, and with him the Rebbetzin. He wanted to go once again to the wife of the unfortunate man, and the Rebbetzin would not absent herself from a place where help and comfort were needed. Near the great fountain, called the *Kashte*, next to the city hall, the rabbi was detained by some members of his congregation. Everyone was eager to hear something about the day's happenings directly from his mouth. At the same time the mayor and two aldermen came down the steps of the city hall. When they noticed Dr. Merzbach, they went up to him to tell him that it had just been decided to let the water off at the dam early the next morning, through the large sluice, in order, if possible, to recover the corpse of Teacher Sandberg; for it was not likely that with the water so shallow, the body had been carried down stream; it had probably been caught somewhere in the canal. A shudder ran through the crowd. Those standing near the mayor listened to what he said with bated breath and passed on his words to their neighbors. Like wildfire it spread through the crowd: "To-morrow they'll recover the body of Teacher Sandberg." From the Kashte rose the primitive figure of a Neptune, trident in hand; and the silver moonlight gleamed on the large fountain and the listening throngs about it.

"To-morrow they'll recover the body of Teacher Sandberg."

All of a sudden a shrill cry rang out and was echoed by the mass of human beings, stirred to the highest pitch of excitement. Horror-struck they scattered in confusion and took to their heels, only now and then looking back fearsomely at a gruesome vision which presented itself to their sight. In one second the Ring was vacated, every one had hidden in the houses. There—slowly and meditatively, like a ghost, Teacher Sandberg stalked across the square, in the garb in which the good Lord had created him. He was absolutely naked, not a shred of clothing upon him; his hands at his legs, as though in his usual fashion he were hiding them in trouser pockets, his feet scraping along the ground.

The Ring looked as though it had been swept. Only the rabbi, the two trustees, the mayor, the aldermen, and the Rebbetzin remained at the Kashte. The Rebbetzin, when the singular figure approached, faced about in confusion and eagerly contemplated the Neptune, who, although a river god, wore much more clothing than Teacher Sandberg. The moonlight glistened on the trident and bathed the entire tragi-comic scene in its pale light. The teacher shuffled close up to the gentlemen, who regarded him with glances of astonishment mixed with disapproval. Was this object Sandberg or his ghost? How could he be wandering about through the city across the Ring past all these people in so scanty a costume? The thing was unheard of; the like of it had never been seen. Presumably the man was dead, and here he was strolling about—and in what a state!

Some of the bolder spirits crept out of their houses again, and here and there a curious face bobbed up behind the window panes. The situation was tense. The Rebbetzin still had her back turned to the group; and the Neptune looked very shy, as if to say: "We barbarians are better people after all; none of us would dare saunter about the Ring in bright moonlight without a shred of clothing on."

Finally the rabbi recovered enough self-possession to address the man standing before him in the garb in which the Lord had fashioned him.

"Is that you, Sandberg?" he asked in a tone of mingled severity and mildness.

"Yes, Herr Rabbiner, it's I," came the plaintive reply.

"Your wife, your children, the congregation, the city, all are mourning you as dead."

"God forbid!" the teacher exclaimed. "Why should I be dead? I am alive, Herr Rabbiner, praised be God, even if something very disagreeable did happen to me."

"He will catch cold, if he doesn't look out." Shmul Eisner, who had come up in the meantime, tossed the joke to another bystander. But no one thought of offering the naked man a bit of clothing. The amazement was still too great. So the audience was continued, and Teacher Sandberg, in the primitive garb in which he was, related his adventure before a college of judges consisting of the rabbinate and the municipal authorities.

In the morning he had gone to take a bath, and had undressed behind some bushes at the edge of the stream near the Petershof dam, where not a soul passes at that hour of the day. He dived into the refreshing depths. The water was delicious. Forgotten the torturing heat, forgotten the hunger and thirst of the fast day! He struck off down stream and let himself be carried along by the soft waves, gently warmed and brightened by the sun. After half an hour, possibly longer, he swam back to the spot where he had undressed—but horror of horrors! his clothes had disappeared. Not a thing had been left behind, not even a shirt to cover his body. Utterly distraught, he ran up and down the bank, hunting for his clothes, calling, crying out, imploring, beseeching help from somewhere. Nothing stirred. Had someone played a trick on him? Had tramps passed by and taken the clothes along as profitable booty? He was absolutely ignorant of how the thing had happened. But one thing was clear; he must hide himself until night, and then find some way of creeping home. He reckoned on the probability that the people, tired out by the fast, would go to bed earlier than usual. So, resigned and thoroughly worn out by the excitement of the fearful adventure, he slid into a field of corn in full ear, ripe for harvesting, and crawled way into its depths to hide himself completely. He dropped down exhausted; the corn-stalks waved high over his head, the crickets chirped, the ragged robins and wild poppies nodded about him. He again began to meditate upon his peculiar position. What happened after that he could not remember. He must have fallen into a deep sleep, and so failed to hear the call of the search parties. When he awoke, the moon was high in the heavens. He did not know what time it was; but he supposed it must be late at night, for he was chilled to the marrow, and dew lay upon the field from which he emerged. Then he wended his way homeward, through the meadows wrapt in solitude and nocturnal quiet. With beating heart he slipped past the houses along the deserted streets. It was like a city of the dead. He thought it must be long past midnight, that everybody was buried in sleep. It could not occur to him that the people, because of his disappearance, had congregated at the Ring. Emboldened by the quiet, he stepped along at a livelier pace, and even calculated that by crossing the Ring and going down Rybniker Street he could reach his home sooner. He was not in the least afraid of meeting anyone at that time except the nightwatch, to whom he could easily explain his plight. So he came through a narrow side street, which ran from the Flour Market and opened right on the Ring and landed—where his appearance was welcomed as a ghost by the excited crowd. And now he was standing before the gentlemen, and he could not have done otherwise, so help him God—Amen!

His savior in need was the Rebbetzin. With averted face she listened to the half-comic, half-pitiful narrative, and suddenly she let her large black mantilla fall to the ground behind her. Shmul Eisner, who noticed the act, and immediately perceived its purpose, sprang forward, picked up the shawl, and hung it about the teacher's trembling limbs. Then, draped in the Rebbetzin's black mantilla, the teacher was led to the shelter of his home, to wife and child.

"Won't Frau Teacher Sandberg be jealous, though," exclaimed Reb Shmul, the joker, "when she sees him coming home with nothing on but the mantilla of the Rebbetzin."

"The chief thing is, he is here," replied his companion. And that is what the whole congregation thought, when it sought its well-deserved rest.

OCTOBER 6.

My position keeps me very busy. In a mining district accidents occur almost daily. Besides, the whisky fiend has to be reckoned with, leading, as it does, to all sorts of excesses, brawls, and murderous assaults. Scarcely a day passes but that I have to make trips into the country, which offers small cheer now in the grey autumn weather and in this dispiriting region. My disposition, naturally inclined to be sombre, becomes still more melancholy; and when I ride through the rain-soaked country, past forges, furnaces, and culm heaps, covered with a thick pall of smoke, with the immediate prospect of seeing dead or injured victims, and having to set down a record of human misery and woe, my mood becomes ever blacker and blacker. I never find time to attend to patients among the upper classes. I believe I am given up as a hopeless case—a Jewish Kreisphysikus, sans wife, who doesn't seek introductions, must be either an abnormality or a capricious, stuck-up fool, at any rate a person not to be reckoned with seriously. My colleagues probably have the same opinion of me. After the inevitable initial formalities, I did not come in contact with them; if chance brings us together, we give each other a cool if courteous greeting.

This exclusiveness has its advantages. The time left free from my duties belongs to me entirely, and I do not spend it thriftlessly in society to which I am indifferent. It has not been my experience that intercourse with many people is of any profit. One gets so little, and gives so much, much too much of what is best and noblest in one's nature, especially if one is a man of feeling, intellect, and ardent temperament. The strongest chord is almost never touched. In the most favorable circumstances, the exchange of courtesies is purely formal, and the acts of friendship are entirely perfunctory. These merely external amenities make men vulgar and untrue, I would not like to use an even stronger expression and say dishonest. Heine's words occur to me:

Weisse, höfliche Manschetten,

Ach wenn sie nur Herzen hätten,

Herzen in der Brust und Liebe,—wahre Liebe in den Herzen,

Denn mich tötet ihr Gesinge von erlogenen Liebesschmerzen.

Perhaps such principles produce loneliness; but they strengthen one; at all events they do not embitter the mind and spirit, as some maintain. I have never been sadder than in the midst of many people, among whom I did not find—one human being! And nothing has a happier influence on me than to find a human being where I least expect one—Simon Eichelkatz, for example.

Yesterday, after an interval of several days, I went to see him late in the evening. I was worn out and unnerved by my official visit to a neighboring place, the centre of the Silesian coal-mining district. Two workmen had gotten into a fight in a tavern, and the host, in trying to separate them and smooth over their differences, himself became enraged and threw out the more aggressive of the two. The reeling, sodden wretch lost his balance, and, tumbling down the steps, knocked his head on a stone. His skull was crushed, and he died in a few minutes from contusion of the brain. When I reached the spot, a mob of wild, excited forms had gathered about the scene of the drama. Policemen stood on guard; and a cloth covered the corpse, which was not to be disturbed until after an inspection by the officials of the locality. I could do nothing more than affirm that the victim was dead, the examination showed that death had occurred as a result of a fall caused by violent mishandling. The author of the deed was a Jew. He was immediately imprisoned, and with great difficulty was withdrawn from the summary lynch-justice of the enraged crowd. Defrauded of the prisoner, they turned against his family and his property. The windows of his house were smashed in; the shop was utterly destroyed, and the whisky—that ruinous, unholy "dispeller of cares "—flowed from the casks into the street. His wife and children tried to save their goods and possessions from the fury of the vandals, but received kicks and blows for their efforts. It was a horrid scene. The policemen did not succeed in restoring order and quiet for some time. Is it possible they had not received sufficient power from the authorities? Was there some other reason? At any rate I had to interpose and try to allay the turmoil. At last the crowd dispersed; but ever and again the echo reached my ears of assassin—murderer—Jew—assassin—dirty thief—cheat—Jew—Jew—liar.

All this had utterly depressed and unnerved me. I really wanted to stay at home; but I reconsidered and decided it was better to substitute a pure, peaceful picture for these torturing impressions, and I went to my old friend. I found him gay and friendly as ever, despite the lateness of the hour. But my mood did not escape his searching gaze; and on his questioning me, I told him what had happened. As was his wont, he rubbed his forehead with his forefinger and thumb, and looked thoughtfully into space. Finally he said:

"That's the way it is to-day, and that's the way it's always been. If a man of some other religion commits a wrong, it's a bad man that did it; but if it happens among our people, then it's the 'Jew'! That's a bitter pill we have to swallow, Herr Doktor, a very bitter pill. But it *is* so, and it doesn't change, even though the world is said to be so cultured and progressive, and humane—the Jew remains a Jew! In the eyes of the *Goy* he's something peculiar, something disgraceful! And for that reason the Jews must stick to the Jew; because the others don't, and never did, and never will. We have nothing to expect or hope from them—and we needn't be afraid of them, neither, we Jews, if we stick together. Then, if something should happen as to-day, Herr Kreisphysikus, it's a misfortune, but not a calamity. Because the man who did it, is a wicked brute who by accident is a Jew, and might just as well have been a Goy. What has religion to do with these matters, anyhow? Does a Goy do something bad because he's a Christian, or a Jew because he's an Israelite? Religion teaches both of them to be good, upright, and pious; and if they aren't, how can religion help it? Religion is not to be blamed; only good can result from religion. Whether Jew or Christian, it remains the same. Each can learn from his own religion; for there is something moral in every religion; and for that reason everybody should honor his own religion and stick to it. The deeds of men must be judged according to the nature of each man, not according to his religion. Because, if the Jew at Raudnitz chucked out the *Shikker* so roughly that he died, the Jew did it because he has an angry, wild, ungovernable temper. Do you suppose he was thinking of his religion? If he only had! The Shikker would be alive if he had. Because the Jewish belief forbids the Jew to be sinful or violent, and to kill; just as their belief forbids the Goyim. And the world won't be better until all understand that a man must have respect for his neighbor, because he is a man. When each and everyone feels that he is master of his honor and his dignity, he will also find his rights—not as a Jew and not as a Christian, but as a man!"

I stared at the old man fixedly. Whence these ideas on the rights and dignity of man? Whence these opinions animated by the spirit of humanitarianism? Here, in the Jewish community? If he had suddenly begun to unriddle the problem of "the thing in itself," I should scarcely have been astonished. Notions had arisen in the mind of this simple man, on the philosophy of human rights and the philosophy of religion, worthy of a great scholar, although he had never heard a word of the notable thinkers who had constructed these ideas into an enduring cosmic edifice.

OCTOBER 11.

The affair in Raudnitz had a sad sequel, and gave me a great deal to do. The prisoner hanged himself in jail. The coroner's inquest and the attendant formalities occupied most of my time. I was compelled to drive repeatedly to Raudnitz, and I became acquainted with the unfortunate family of the accused who had taken justice into his own hands. The wife, well-mannered, had a rather hard expression; the two daughters were educated and well-bred; the aged mother of the man was pathetic in her old Jewish humility and pious resignation. A fearful fate had overtaken the unsuspecting folk who a few days before had been living in quiet happiness. I asked the woman what could possibly have driven her husband to his desperate deed. In the most unfavorable circumstances he would have been punished for homicide through carelessness, and the sentence would certainly have been light, since he could have proved that the fatal fall of the victim was primarily due to his drunkenness.

"But the shame, Herr Doktor, the shame. For months he would have been in jail undergoing examination and cross-questioning; then he'd surely have remained in prison a couple of years—for they would never have acquitted him entirely. He didn't want to live through all that—the shame, Herr Kreisphysikus, shame before his children, and the sorrow for his mother. It would have lasted years, long, long years; and so he ended it at one stroke. He knew me, and he felt sure I wouldn't lose my head, and would provide for the children. He was certain of it, and knew he would be a greater burden to his family if he was buried alive in prison than if lying dead beneath the earth. It is terribly painful, but there is an end of it; the other would have been an eternal shame. That is the way he reasoned; he killed himself for the sake of his children."

I shuddered, when I heard the affair discussed so rationally and cold-bloodedly. Was it heartlessness or keensightedness that made them so hard and unloving? Hadn't the woman loved and respected her husband? Yet did she not judge his deed as the outcome of reasoned consideration, his voluntary death as a sacrifice to his family, as a martyr's death?

A question rose to my lips.

"But tell me, my dear Mrs. Schlochauer, your husband must surely have thought that he would hurt you deeply, you with whom he lived happily and whom he certainly loved and respected. And he must have felt that he would give his old mother infinite pain."

An odd smile drew the corners of her mouth, and some moments passed before she roused herself from a sort of trance, and said: "His mother is very old, Herr Doktor, eighty-two years old; she hasn't much more to expect from life, I am sure he thought of that. And as for his love for me "—she hesitated—"he was always considerate of me, and respectful, but love? In a decent Jewish family the love of man and wife is their love for their children."

What had moved the soul of this woman to such conclusions on married life?

Yesterday I learned by chance that she was the daughter of a teacher in Beuthen, and had herself been trained as a teacher. The community had granted her a scholarship, to complete her course for the teacher's examinations at the Seminary in Breslau. There she became acquainted with a young painter, a Christian, and a love affair, as pure as it was ardent, developed between them. When her parents heard of the affair, they made her come home immediately. Her studies were interrupted, and she took up life again in her parents' house, the fountain of her emotions sealed, the bitter sorrow of an unhappy love swelling her heart. What was her inner development after this first, hard disillusionment, this spiritual conflict? Who can tell?

When, some years later, the first flush of youth past, her father expressed to her his wish that she marry Schlochauer in Raudnitz, the well-to-do proprietor of a distillery, in order to lighten his own troubles in bringing up his numerous offspring, she obeyed without a murmur. Her husband respected her, and offered no objection to her assisting her family and so enabling her brothers to study. He loved her, too—for she presented him with four children. Two died young—and as for the two remaining daughters, she would provide for them carefully. Her husband would not be deceived in her; the sacrifice of his life was not made in vain.

"When everything is settled, Herr Kreisphysikus, I am going to sell the business and the house, and move to Berlin. We have some means, Herr Doktor; my husband was a good manager. In Berlin we are not well known; and grass grows over everything that happens. No matter if a person here and there knows something about it; it is quickly forgotten. People have no time there to gossip about private affairs. I have three brothers in Berlin, all in respected positions. So, in the large city, I shall live free from care with my daughters; they are still young and will get over the pain and horror of the present."

"And you, Frau Schlochauer?" I hastily asked.

"I? I shall do my duty."

The words sounded so natural, yet it made a painful impression on me to see how collected she was, how quietly and circumspectly she looked into the future from out of the confusion and distress of the moment. Perhaps she divined the course of my thoughts, for suddenly she continued:

"Don't wonder that I speak of this matter so calmly. You become accustomed to such things if for twenty years you live with a business man in this neighborhood, among such rude, rough folk. You learn to be on the lookout, to be careful and practical. And you forget that once you regarded the world with different eyes."

She uttered the last words softly, with downward glance. When I heard the history of her youth yesterday, I saw her in my mind's eye again, and a feeling of boundless pity for this woman swept over me—not for what she was suffering now—now that she was steeled and experienced—but for her youth, the youth she had lost because practical considerations and hindrances determined the course of her life.

But now I must tell about a remarkable acquaintance I made yesterday, the man who told me what I know of Frau Schlochauer's history. He introduces some humor into the affair.

"Herr Jonas Goldstücker."

The visiting card with this name printed in large Roman characters lies before me and seems to throw a crafty and comical smile at me. In fact my new acquaintance is very amusing. The card was brought in to me at the end of my afternoon office hours. Herr Jonas Goldstücker! I thought it was a patient, and had him admitted even though the time for receiving patients was past. A few moments later an elderly man sat before me, well-preserved and decently dressed. He was perfectly open in letting his curious gaze rove through my room, and I felt that in a minute period of time he had a thorough survey. His inventory took in all the objects in the room, myself included. His sly eyes seemed ever to be investigating and inspecting, and although he frequently pressed them shut, or glanced into space over his nickel-plated *pince-nez*, one felt correctly catalogued and pigeonholed. Herr Jonas Goldstücker began to interest me. Without waiting for me to ask his business, he said:

"I knew, Herr Kreisphysikus, that you always stay at home a little while after your office hours, and that's the reason I chose this time for coming to you; I thought we would not be disturbed now."

So he was acquainted with my habits, with something about my private life; he wanted to speak to me without outside interruption—did this man know of some secret? Did a matter calling for discretion lead him to me? But he gave me no time for surmise, and added:

"You certainly don't run after practice among well-to-do patients; no one can reproach you with that—you live like a hermit; and outside of Simon Eichelkatz no one has had the honor of seeing you at his home."

My face must have looked very stupid, or it must have expressed great amazement at his intimate tone and his familiarity with my affairs; because he laughed and said:

"Yes, Herr Kreisphysikus, in a little town you get to know people, and all about them."

"But I don't know *you*," I interrupted, my patience at last exhausted.

"I am Jonas Goldstücker."

"So your card tells me. But I should like to permit myself the question, to what I owe the honor of your visit."

"O, you'll soon find out, Herr Kreisphysikus. I am not sick, as you see. Quite another reason brings me to you. But if I should need medical advice, I shall not fail to come to you, although Sanitätsrat Ehrlich has been treating me for six years—since the time his daughter Annie married Herr Rechtsanwalt Bobrecker of Leobschütz. An excellent match. Any day Bobrecker might have gotten sixty thousand marks, and Löwenberg, the wool manufacturer in Oppeln, would have given him as much as seventy-five thousand, but he wanted to marry a girl from an educated family, and no other. Well, the daughter of Sanitätsrat Ehrlich is no vain delusion."

My breath was completely taken away by this information regarding private matters.

Next came the abrupt question:

"In general, Herr Kreisphysikus, are you in favor of wet or dry treatment in rheumatism?"

A patient after all! I breathed more freely. Herr Jonas Goldstücker had given me a creepy sensation.

"I don't understand what you mean by that."

"I mean, are you in favor of massage and electricity or in favor of baths?"

The impudent assurance of the question utterly astounded me, and I wanted to give him a brusque reply, when he continued:

"Sanitätsrat Ehrlich is an excellent physician; but he's a bit antiquated already, Herr Kreisphysikus. The young doctors of to-day make a much more lymphatic impression."

Doubtless, he meant "emphatic," because a few moments later another pretentious word was incorrectly applied.

"But Sanitätsrat Ehrlich after all has the largest practice in the congregation; and people would look on it as bigamy if anyone were to say anything against him."

I was only slightly acquainted with my colleague, and I did not know that doubt of his powers would be regarded as blasphemy—probably what Jonas Goldstücker meant to say. The humor of the situation at last began to dawn upon me, and I awaited the further utterances of my remarkable guest in amused curiosity.

"And his house, Herr Kreisphysikus, his house! Really, very fine. The Frau Sanitätsträtin knows how to do the honors and to keep her distance."

What he meant by this was not exactly clear to me; but I learned that the youngest daughter of my colleague Ehrlich was a ravishing maiden, as Herr Jonas Goldstücker assured me.

"Very highly educated, speaks every language, plays the piano as well as Leubuscher (I didn't know of the performer), and only Chopin, Rubinstein, Offenbach, Brahm."

"Brahms, Herr Goldstücker, Brahms."

"Why, yes, I said Brahm, Herr Kreisphysikus. And what she doesn't know, besides! And quite a housekeeper, too; she learned cooking. No, not a soul can find a thing to say against Miss Edith—Edith, a pretty name, Herr Kreisphysikus, Edith."

He was silent for a moment. I was on the point of telling him that all this had very little interest for me, and that he should come to the real object of his visit; but he continued to impress me as a man of the better classes, with fairly decent manners, calling for a certain amount of consideration. So I maintained my attitude of expectancy, and listened to his digressions and discourses on this theme and that. In the course of his remarks he exclaimed:

"It's really a shame that you don't visit at Sanitätsrat Ehrlich's, though I can imagine you haven't very much time. And now you must be having a good deal of annoyance with that affair in Raudnitz. A terrible misfortune, terrible. That Herr Schlochauer must have had a fearful temper; because it isn't so easy to throw a man out of your place and kill him outright. It must be very trying to his wife; she is an educated woman, daughter of the teacher Weiss, in Beuthen. She never thought she would marry a thoroughly uneducated saloon-keeper. But he got along very well, and you never heard any talk about her not living happily with him. She always had what she needed, and much more. She could help her own family and give her two daughters a good education—very different from what would have happened if she'd gotten her painter. What a sad picture they'd have made, she and her picture-maker."

He laughed complacently at his pun, and I meditated over the ideal Jewish marriage. Then I was made acquainted with the story of Frau Rosalie Schlochauer's youthful love.

"But that he should have gone and taken his life! It's really awful to bring about a misfortune so deliberately. However, a sister-in-law of Frau Schlochauer, a cousin of my wife, married to the book-dealer Grosser, told me that the widow is remarkably calm. Frau Grosser herself is half dead from the excitement, and she can't possibly comprehend how Frau Schlochauer can be so collected. The idea of hanging himself in prison! Absurd! If he had waited, for all we know he might have been set free. At any rate he would not have gotten more than three or four years. In no circumstances would he have been put into the penitentiary. Herr Rechtsanwalt Cassirer told me yesterday that the jury would certainly have agreed on *dolus eventualiter.*"

Of course, what Herr Jonas Goldstücker wanted to say was *dolus eventualis.* But a little thing like that didn't matter to him, and I continued to wonder how he came to know everybody and associate with the best families. He was evidently on a most intimate footing with the heads of the community.

"Frau Schlochauer," he said, after a while, "will doubtless move away from Raudnitz. Life for her there in these circumstances is impossible. And what should she do with two daughters, who are almost grown up and will soon be marriageable? She will certainly go to Berlin. Her brothers live there; one of them is a lawyer, another is a physician, and the third owns a large shirtwaist factory. There she will have someone to cling to."

I had a mental picture of Frau Schlochauer, quiet in her grief, earnest, thoughtful, as she unfolded to me her plans for the future. And this man knew it all. He had guessed it and now expressed his opinion on events in the life of a stranger.

"In Berlin people don't bother about such stories. There Frau Schlochauer is the sister of the lawyer Weiss and the doctor Weiss; she is the rich Frau Schlochauer with two pretty, well-bred daughters. That's enough. The girls will make very good matches. They say the property amounts to a great deal, much more than you'd think by looking at Herr Schlochauer. There he was working all day and thinking of nothing but how to serve his customers. He left culture and education to his wife—and now the money, in addition. The sale of the big house and the distillery may bring in as much as four hundred thousand marks. Yesterday Rothmann, the banker, told me Schlochauer had been well off, almost rich. Some of his money he placed with Rothmann, the rest with the Breslau Diskonto Bank; and Rothmann knows the amount of his deposits. If Frau Schlochauer, when the time comes, will give each daughter one hundred thousands marks—for the present she won't use more than the interest on her money—she will be able to do very well with them. Of course, she won't get the sort of person that looks out for a so-called fine family. People like that ask after every possible thing, and are sure to find out about the detention in prison and the suicide. There are some who won't suffer the tiniest speck on the family name—but there are enough young people, too, who haul in without questioning and think, 'Let by-gones be by-gones.' Sometimes even physicians and lawyers aren't so particular about 'antecedents.'"

I looked at my watch. The act should have been an indication to him that I was getting impatient, and was displeased with the familiarity of his talk; but he seemed not to comprehend the delicate hint. For he suddenly broke out with:

"Herr Rabbiner Grünbaum in Loslau was a brother of your mother, wasn't he, Herr Kreisphysikus? I knew him very well. I'm from Loslau, too. A fine man, and very good and friendly. He was very much loved in the Khille, and my blessed mother always used to say: 'Fine as silk, fine as silk.' I knew your father, too, Herr Kreisphysikus; once when he was in Loslau, at the funeral of your uncle, I saw him, and I heard the sermon he delivered. Great, really great! So touching! The whole congregation shed tears. Your father must have been a splendid pulpit orator. A pity he was in such a small congregation. He belonged in Breslau or Berlin. But, God bless me, good can be accomplished in the smallest of places; and he certainly did do good. Herr Doktor Feilchenstein was in Johannisbad with me this summer, and he couldn't get through telling me about your parents, Herr Kreisphysikus, and what a pious, good old lady your mother is. No wonder, either, if she's a sister of Herr Rabbiner Grünbaum, of Loslau. And Doktor Feilchenstein told me of you, too. You know, I mean your cousin from Frankfort-on-the-Oder. When he heard that I was from Raudnitz, he asked after you, and sent his regards. He refused to believe that I hadn't met you, when you'd been here since April. But, dear me, in summer everybody, of course, is away, and it's no time for visiting. But now, Herr Kreisphysikus, it's October already, and you haven't made any visits yet."

What gave the man the right to remonstrate with me on this subject? To be sure, he seemed well acquainted with my family affairs—my cousin sent messages by him. I pondered a while; the name "Jonas Goldstücker" was not on my visiting list. Curious! All I said was: "You must leave me to judge of that."

"But I beg of you, Herr Kreisphysikus, you misunderstand me. I assure you I did not mean to instruct you in matters of social form. How could you think such a thing? All I meant was, how should families here get to know and appreciate you, if you keep yourself at such a distance? And your cousin, Doctor Feilchenstein, told me what an excellent person you are, how earnest and thorough, and how you had opened up a career for yourself when you were comparatively young. Not out of the thirties and a Physikus already—and how much pleasure you are giving your old mother."

Since I last saw my cousin he must have developed into a garrulous old woman. What had possessed him to tell an utter stranger so much of my life, to praise me, and speak of my relations with my quiet, reserved little mother? I couldn't believe my ears, and I was about to give expression to my amazement when he continued:

"And how happy your dear mother would be if you would soon present her with a nice daughter-in-law! If the girl is fine and educated, your mother might even live with you, and end her days under your roof. Many young girls, to be sure, are not in favor of such an arrangement; but that depends, and Edith Ehrlich is such a clever person...."

I jumped from my seat, and came near laughing out loud. At last the mystery was solved. Herr Jonas Goldstücker, who honored me with so curious and intimate a visit, was a *Shadchen*, the marriage broker of the congregation!

It was highly entertaining. But apparently he did not care to notice that I took the matter as a joke, for he remained quietly seated and continued:

"And Herr Sanitätsrat prefers a physician, who might take up his practice later...."

"Marry into the profession, so to speak," I interjected.

"Yes, Herr Kreisphysikus. But that's only by the way. In addition he will give his daughter fifty thousand marks, just as much as Rechtsanwalt Bobrecker got, and if you—you might pay a visit there anyway—I am sure if you once get to know Miss Edith, you will see that the description I gave of her is true from head to foot. She has a beautiful head of chestnut brown hair...."

The association of ideas was delicious.

"She has a fine figure, medium size, and when I think how glad your old mother would be...."

I do not know whether I politely showed Herr Jonas Goldstücker the door, or whether he went voluntarily. At all events he was gone. But this very day I mean to write a letter to my cousin, Doktor Feilchenstein, and give him a piece of my mind.

OCTOBER 10.

"Do you know what a *Roshekol* is?" Simon Eichelkatz asked me with a mischievous smile, when I visited him this afternoon.

"A Roshekol is the head of a congregation," I answered. He laughed a gentle, chuckling laugh, which was the usual expression of good temper with him, and said:

"A Roshekol is a disagreeable fellow."

"But not always, Herr Eichelkatz?"

"Almost always, at least if you get your idea of him from the rabbi and the cantor, nebbich, or even from the Khille in general. He is generally arrogant, disputatious, autocratic, and ambitious. As he hasn't anything else to rule, he wants to rule the congregation at least, and he insists the poor officials shall depend upon his good-will entirely. He suffers no contradiction, and as for the opinion of another, it doesn't occur to him that it is entitled to any respect. He commands and the others must agree with him. For they are nearly all dependent upon him, and, therefore, are either for or with him. On the one side is his *Mishpocheh*, on the other, people who stand in business or personal relations with him. If he happens to have a so-called academic education, matters are still worse, because on the strength of it he and the Khille as well put on an extra touch of pride. He has some standing in the city, too, is on good terms with the Goyim, and is generally a city alderman. This makes a tremendous impression on the Khille, and it doesn't occur to the *Narronim* that they themselves made him alderman. They say with pride: 'Our Roshekol must be a very intelligent man; he's an alderman also!' The Roshekol, it is true, usually is an intelligent person; but he lacks character and genuine goodness and humanity. It's all on the surface—fine phrases, long words, but within cold, hollow, and calculating. All he thinks of is to show himself off in the best light and hurt other people's feelings."

I shook my finger at Simon laughingly and said:

"Reb Shimme, I think you are looking at things through dark spectacles; they can't be so bad as you paint them."

"Just live in a Khille fifty years, and you'll know whether or not I'm exaggerating. If you'd have known the president of the congregation, Krakauer, *Doktor* Krakauer, saving your reverence, you'd have said at least what I say, that a Roshekol is a disagreeable fellow. Perhaps you'd have said even more. Lots of people in the Khille were vexed at his treatment of the poor officials, nebbich, and made a fist at him behind his back. But they were too weak to do anything. I, too, Herr Kreisphysikus. What can a single person do? But when I think of it even now, my gall rises."

"Now, now, my dear Reb Shimme, if you excite yourself, I won't allow you to speak one word about it." I tried to soothe him.

"Why? If one speaks from the heart, it doesn't hurt. Just let me tell you quietly about Herr Doktor Krakauer, saving your reverence. I won't make it a reproach against him that he came of a thoroughly ordinary family. There are many Jews of low extraction who work themselves up into a fine, noble manhood. Besides, if we recall our common stock, everyone is justified in regarding himself as a nobleman of the most ancient lineage. But then one should act accordingly, which most of us unfortunately fail to do. Herr Doktor Krakauer, saving your reverence, certainly did not behave like a nobleman. His father was a dealer in raw hides in Peiskretscham, an industrious, decent sort of a Jew, who couldn't read or write. His mother was a simple woman, formerly the cook at Herr Bernhard Markus's. They were not young when they married, and when a son was born to them, they were overjoyed. They decided to make something remarkable of the child. The parents now had only one aim, and the boy, who was a studious pupil, made it possible for them to fulfil their desire. He was to study, become an educated, learned gentleman, a doctor. Whatever the dealer in raw hides and his wife lacked, was to appear in the son, and more, too. And they lived to experience the joy of seeing him ashamed of them. After he had taken up the profession of physician, and had received positions of trust in the city and the congregation, he was very careful to keep the dealer in raw hides and the Jewish cook hidden away. He was their son on the quiet and in secret. To be known as their son might have hurt him in the eyes of the world, and reflect on his public position. So the two old people, who had worked untiringly day and night to put their only child on a higher level than themselves, could watch the results of their efforts only from afar. For his greed, his energy, his cunning, and his disregard of other people had actually advanced him to a dazzling height. He married into a well-to-do family; but the girl was so shy and stupid that she yielded to his autocratic will, in constant terror lest she displease him.

"Now, then, Herr Kreisphysikus, imagine such a man a Roshekol for years. He oppressed and injured the whole Khille; it didn't have the courage to oppose him. Everyone trembled before him. The old janitor of the synagogue, the Shabbes Goy Marek, who died last year, always used to say: 'When Krakauer comes to Shul, holding his head so high you'd think he was trying to bump against the *Mogen Dovid*, and expanding his chest as if to beat for *Al Chet* upon it, the whole Khille trembles, because he's so swell and eats *Trefa*, and treats the people like cattle.' Marek was right, he was a sensible man. And more than the members of the Khille, nebbich, those who were dependent upon him trembled before him. But two people did not tremble, Rabbi Doktor Merzbach, who was too aristocratic by nature, and still less, the 'haughty Rebbetzin,' who openly called Doktor Krakauer an upstart, and returned his greeting so condescendingly that he always took the other side of the street when he saw her coming. By way of return he never failed when the occasion offered to do harm to the rabbi and wound his feelings.

"His desire for vengeance was incredible; and the more he tried to keep it from showing in his outward manners, the more it fermented in his coarse-grained heart; and wherever it was possible to injure Doktor Merzbach, he did it. No one seeing the tall, heavily-built, broad-shouldered man with his ingratiating smile, his assumption of aristocracy, and his courtly manners, would have supposed his exterior concealed so black a soul. Well, his day of reckoning came after all. But in the meantime he continued to gain influence; and he also had an excellent practice, which later, to be sure, was sliced away a bit by Sanitätsrat Ehrlich. May no one suffer the fate they invoked on each other—but before the world the best of friends. On one point they were always agreed, to worry and annoy those who were under their control, the officials of the congregation, nebbich! Herr Sanitätsrat Ehrlich was also a trustee; and the two ruled in the congregation for more than thirty years. The first ugly trick they played on Dr. Merzbach was at the dedication of the New Synagogue. I think I've told you about it already, Herr Kreisphysikus. The building of the New Synagogue was due entirely to Dr. Merzbach's efforts. Who would have paid any attention to Herr Dr. Krakauer, saving your reverence? Dr. Merzbach's name had a good sound, and one is not a son-in-law of Reb Salme Friedländer of Posen for nothing. That's exactly what Dr. Krakauer, saving your reverence, could not forgive him, although he always performed his difficult duties quietly and simply. The Rebbetzin, it is true, very clearly showed what she thought of the son of Isaac Krakauer, dealer in raw hides, and Frau Yetta, once cook at the house of Bernhard Markus. There's no denying it, the Rebbetzin was proud. But in spite of that she was charitable and noble, and all the poor people in the community loved her. She stood at the beds of the sick and the dying. In the awful cholera time she courageously went with her husband from place to place, showing no sign of fear. She brought comfort to the sufferers, and took the helpless and the orphaned under her wing. It was only to people like Krakauer that she showed her scorn for upstarts, if, as she said, they did not also elevate their minds and their morals. You can imagine, Herr Kreisphysikus, that there were always 'decent' people in the Khille who reported to the president every word the Rebbetzin said, only exaggerated and adorned with extra flourishes. There were two especially, fine men, Herr Meyer Nathanson and Herr Saul Feuerstein. Nathanson was the *Shammes* and treasurer of the Khille. He was called the 'Caretaker of the Khille,' because he concerned himself about everything, and was Dr. Krakauer's right-hand man. Feuerstein was a well-known *Pleitegeher*, a professional bankrupt, and made a good living from his profession. These two men acted as spies to ferret out and report every word, every act of Frau Dr. Merzbach's. She didn't concern herself about them; and sometimes she may have been glad that the people learned what she thought of them. But there was always some disturbance and annoyance; and finally the good Herr Rabbiner was the one to suffer. I can scarcely get myself to speak to you about the way Dr. Krakauer, saving your reverence, and his assistants imposed their will on the meetings of the committee, and how, when the New Synagogue stood there completed, all the difficulties overcome, they sent for a rabbi from Berlin to hold the dedication speech. Did you ever hear of such a thing? As though a rabbi were a prima donna! He comes and preaches the dedication sermon and pushes aside our own rabbi! Dr. Krakauer, and Meyer Nathanson, the caretaker of the Khille, and Saul Feuerstein, the professional bankrupt, triumph; and with them the 'Saints,' whom the whole business of the New Synagogue doesn't suit anyhow. I believe Dr. Merzbach suffered very much at the time; his feelings must have been bitterly hurt; but he did not complain, and he did not lose his joy in his work. When he stood in the pulpit on the first Shabbes after the dedication, and thanked God for having permitted the congregation to erect their new house of worship, and also thanked the congregation for having made sacrifices and patiently awaited the completion of the difficult work, which he recommended to their protection, their fidelity, and their piety, as a place of upliftment, of edification, comfort, and faith, the eyes of all were filled with tears, and everyone felt that the real dedication sermon had not been delivered until that Shabbes. Marek, the janitor of the synagogue and Shabbes Goy, said that when the people came out of the synagogue, they nodded significantly to one another: 'Even if the other man did come from Berlin he's not a Dr. Merzbach.' But what they said in an undertone, was publicly declared by the Rebbetzin when she left the synagogue, proudly drawing up the black mantilla that had once been draped about the shoulders of Teacher Sandberg:

"'The dedication of the New Synagogue did not take place until to-day, praised be God, through the efforts of him who for ten years spent his whole strength for the success of the work.'

"She said this as she stood on the top of the steps leading down from the side portal to the street; and so loud that the 'caretaker of the Khille,' who was standing near the steps, could hear the words, probably was intended to hear them. By the afternoon he had already reported them to the president, and the result was that the deputy to the convention soon after held in Berlin was not the rabbi, but Herr Dr. Krakauer, saving your reverence, and two other ignorant *Amrazim*."

"That's what you call punishment for the sake of discipline," I interpolated laughingly.

"I don't know what you call it, but I know it's a shame that so large a congregation as ours should not have been represented at the convention by its rabbi, a fine Talmid Chochom, with a good name of the greatest Yichus, but by an *Amhorez* who did not know more of *Yiddishkeit* than a coarse dealer in hides and a Jewish cook could show him."

He came to a sudden stop.

"It sickens me and makes my gall rise to think of these things, Herr Kreisphysikus. And I had to look on and let it all happen, because I was weak and without influence. Nothing could be done."

A thoughtful, wearied look came into his eyes. I seized the moment to take leave, because, in spite of my interest in his narratives, I did not want him to exert himself any more for the present. Outside I advised Feiwel Silbermann to see to it that his master go to bed as soon as possible.

OCTOBER 18.

At last I have learned something of Simon Eichelkatz's life history. As if utterly forgetful of himself, he ransacked the store-house of his brain for recollections of the past, but since his own life was closely bound up with that of the congregation, he came to speak of himself involuntarily. I admit, that without wishing to be indiscreet I brought him to do it. For greatly as the figures and events he describes interest me, yet they belong in the past and have an historical significance. But this old man rises out of the past, as a passive observer, it is true, more than an active doer. Yet, a portion of his being flourishes and develops on the soil of science, in the most modern, most progressive province of spiritual endeavor. What an evolution from Simon Eichelkatz to Friedrich Eichner! I hope to become acquainted with this life which leads from the narrow confines of a Jewish community out into the broad world.

Yesterday my old friend was very talkative. I felt it pleased him to glance back at his own life; and *he* probably felt that it was not vulgar curiosity but true sympathy that led me to him. When I began my diary, I thought it would record the deeds and events of the day happening here, the most recent news; it has turned out to be a book of the recollections of an old man. It's better so. Daily life here is dull and monotonous. The people, as far as I know, seem to be conventional. Those typical characteristics which Simon Eichelkatz reveals to me are lacking in the present generation. The more the Jews are acclimatized, the more they lose of their individuality; and if this is not to be deplored in general, yet it is at the expense of much originality, in both a good and a bad sense. Whatever originality has been saved for present times has taken the form of individualism, which plays a large and significant rôle in modern life; and I believe that if strong individualities are found among Jews, they are traceable to the time when the community at large was concerned with the preservation of individuality and race characteristics. Nowadays the Jews strive for exactly the opposite ideal. But I want to put the past on record. Simon Eichelkatz draws some remarkable though not always agreeable pictures. Yet if viewed in the softening perspective of time and distance, they evoke a feeling of reconciliation and mild tolerance.

Was not an impress laid on the Jews by the narrowness of their life, its one-sided interests, the lack of a wide outlook, and the failure to take a broad view of the world based on fixed ethical principles? Were the large mass of them not rendered doubly small and inferior because the great men among them were entirely too great? Was it not a necessary consequence that crudities and deformities should grow out of these contrasts, which were all the worse because they arose under oppression, in malicious, underhand ways? When I think of it all in the right light, my sympathy overcomes my repugnance for those who in the old communities crucified and burned at the stake the men who furthered the idea of reform in Judaism. Remarkable saints! Meyer Nathanson, the caretaker of the Khille; Saul Feuerstein, the professional bankrupt, and their savory crew, and alongside of them Dr. Krakauer, Dr. Ehrlich, and their colleagues. Alas for the miserable Khilles! Yet I am moved by the recollections of the scenes enacted in the past on this ground where fortune has cast me. Instead of the land of sun, in which the famous ancestor of my great-grandmother in Brody, Dr. Abarbanell, served his Master, the black coals of upper Silesia and the winds of the Beskides; instead of converse with scholars and artists, intercourse with the rude folk here; instead of stimulating activity, dissections and grubbing into the mental state of murderers, perjurers, etc.—such is my life and work; yet I have something to give me inner satisfaction—Simon Eichelkatz.

Yesterday, he said to me: "What the Herr Rabbiner did for the congregation as a whole when he came to this 'black' Khille cannot compare with what he gave to each person separately. He came here in 1849, soon after the great revolution. Shortly before, in the company of a deputation from Posen—he had been rabbi in Unruhstadt—he had stood before the king, in order to give expression to the 'most humble' thanks of the Jews for the rights granted them. You can imagine, Herr Kreisphysikus, how that impressed the people here—a Rav who had stood before the King, a Rav who spoke High German and was a doctor. I tell *you* there was a to-do when they went to receive him and his Rebbetzin; they rode as far as Kandrzin and met him there. Herr Dr. Krakauer, saving your reverence, had then been president for two years, and, to give the devil his due, it was Dr. Krakauer who brought a new Rav here and insisted on his being a man with an academic education. But when he saw that the Rav was independent, and wasn't willing to dance to the tune of his fiddle, he became the Herr Rabbiner's worst enemy. But on the rabbi's arrival Dr. Krakauer delivered the address of welcome in Kandrzin, and rode here in the same carriage with the rabbi and the Rebbetzin. The fourth person in the carriage was the goldsmith Manasse, who was then vice-president, a decent sort of a man. That's the way they entered town; the whole Khille had assembled before the rabbi's house, in the old school building next to the *Mikveh*. Well, and then they went up into his apartments, which had been entirely refurnished by Joseph, the cabinet-maker, and Manasse attempted to deliver a speech there. He was no orator, and embarrassment robbed him of his words. It is reported he stammered so that he couldn't get past the first words, and Dr. Merzbach said: 'Respected friends, I do not need words to be convinced of your sentiment and your kindly feelings for me. I feel that I belong to you, and I came gladly. I hope that in this congregation my activity will find a large field, which perhaps has hitherto been lying fallow, but on which the seeds of fine, noble thoughts, ethical principles, and the idea of forming a worthy communal life, will sprout and bear rich, glorious fruit. I know what you wanted to say to me, respected Herr Vorsteher, even if the emotion of the occasion overpowered you. Whoever looks into your true, good eyes feels that he is facing a kindly man; and so we all have the desire to cling to one another faithfully, and not in words but in deeds work for the weal of this precious congregation.'

"Manasse repeated this speech to me a hundred times. When the reception committee came down to the rest of the people at the end of half an hour, Dr. Krakauer looked so exasperated that Marek, the Shabbes Goy, immediately remarked: 'Something has gotten onto his nerves.' But Saul Feuerstein, professional bankrupt, and later leader of the 'Saints,' did not see why the formation of a 'worthy communal life' was necessary, since they had been *davvening* so long, and everything had been all right. Did he think they had been waiting for him to shape communal life? As for what he said about 'ethical principles,' you'd have to look it up in an encyclopedia before you could understand it. Besides it was a *Chutzpeh* in him to speak of a fallow field. The Khille had managed to exist without a sign of a Dr. Merzbach. Under such auspices the new rabbi assumed office—among Amrazim and coarse fellows, all of them, the well-educated Herr Dr. Krakauer, saving your reverence, and Dr. Ehrlich with his fine ways on top. Only two men understood the rabbi better, Karfunkelstein, the book-dealer, whose father had been rabbi, and Schlesinger, the old iron monger. And then there was another who might have if he had wanted to; a sensible, amiable, good, intelligent, and witty man. He joked about the entire congregation and had a great deal of influence, because they were afraid of his keen judgment. He was the new *Chazen*, the cantor Elias, who had been appointed a short time after the rabbi.

"Now, isn't it so, Herr Kreisphysikus, isn't it more of a misfortune than a shame if one hasn't had the opportunity to learn? But it is a shame if one hasn't respect for the knowledge of others, and if one hurts the feelings of those to whom one should look up with respect. Cantor Elias once said to Dr. Merzbach: 'If you want to remain friends with the Parchonim here, my dear Herr Doktor, you must learn Klabberjas, and Franzefuss, and Sixty-six. Here cards are more important than the pages of the *Gemoreh*.'

"He was right, Herr Kreisphysikus, and the worse he thought and spoke of the people, and the more disrespectfully he treated them, the better they were to him. He could always carry his point. Every year an increase in salary. And they let him do what he wanted. When he stood before the *Omed* on Shabbes and *Yontef* and began to sing, they were all in transports. He sang! Such a voice, such a way of singing! I don't know if there is anything like it now. He touched people to the very marrow of their bones. Perhaps sounds are more affecting than words. What do you think, Herr Kreisphysikus? At any rate he had more influence and power over the Khille than the rabbi. If the rabbi told them something, they had to think about it first; but they only had to hear what the cantor sang to them. Then, after Shul, he went with them to drink a glass of wine at Heimann's, or lunch with them at Schäfer's. Reb Shäfer would stand at the door and declare, when the Herr Kantor came, his heart laughed in his body. When the cantor was present, there was always fun and merriment. He was the most popular man. He would play a little game with the people, he lunched with them, and did not despise Heimann's Hungarian wine. He told the men rugged truths, and he teased the women. No one suspected how genuinely he despised them all, how high he was raised above them. In a few clever words he himself told what he thought about everything.

"'Do you know what our Rav is?' Once when I was present he asked the question of some Baale-Batim with whom he was playing Klabber. 'A pearl cast before swine.'

"'And the Rebbetzin?' some one asked in the midst of their laughter.

"At this he suddenly became quite serious, and said: 'She is a pearl picked from the coronet of a princely family. But you don't understand; why should you? You know *Malkeh* and *Melech* only on cards.' Then he threw down the ace and said: 'I'll take the king and queen with the diamond; they're in better hands than with you.'

"Often he used to say to me: 'You're right, Eichelkatz, for sticking to the rabbi. If anyone can help you, he's the man, for he knows, yes, he knows what is going on in the souls of men—and—the Rebbetzin!'

"And I, I really did need someone who understood what was going on in my soul. I myself hardly understood."

He paused and looked into space, engrossed in thought. I regarded him in silence; then he began with a voice that sounded like an echo from a great distance:

"Do you know what an unhappy marriage is, Herr Kreisphysikus? But how should you? You're a bachelor. You've seen and heard of the thing, but that's nothing. One must live through it oneself, one must experience it in one's own person; then only can you realize that it's the saddest, most fearful thing that can happen to a human being. Both parties are to blame; it's always the fault of both. For neither has the courage to admit the truth, to confess, We've made a mistake; we don't suit each other. They drag through their entire lives in sorrow and deception; and again and again the heart is bruised, and one's own life and the life of others is embittered. And when you finally see into it all, it's too late. When your understanding comes, you're too old. And then you think, it doesn't pay to begin anew for the few years that are left. But the few years are long. Each year has twelve months; each month, thirty days, and some have even thirty-one; each day, twenty-four hours; each hour, sixty minutes; each minute, sixty seconds; and in each second you grieve and fret and live your whole trouble again."

His face took on a thoughtful expression.

"Do you know, Herr Kreisphysikus, they say man's life is short; and what are seventy, or, at the extreme, eighty years in the infinity of time? As a moment. But I tell you, every man who reaches his maturity lives a thousand years, because an entire life is condensed in every moment in which he has an experience. I don't know if you understand me, Herr Doktor. I do not mean those experiences that make up our ordinary life, our habits, and our needs. I mean the things our souls live through. And every sensation of the soul is a whole world in itself, a whole life; everything in us awakens at one blow, and leaps into life, and experiences the entire thing with us. We feel it with all our parts. And now imagine, Herr Kreisphysikus, how many moments each man lives through, how many thousands of lives. This is the standard we should use for measuring our age. And if a man reaches the end of the seventies, like myself, Herr Doktor, and has gone through so many things, his life has not been short, but a thousand years long and more."

Again I stood before the riddle: how did this plain old man arrive at philosophic deductions covering every field of thought, and with singular strength of reasoning lightly solve the most difficult problems, unconsciously, led only by intuition, which clearly and firmly guided him along a path where others groped for the way of truth? Did he not instinctively arrive at the correct thing, when he measured the extent of life by intensity, and not by number of years?

What *had* Simon Eichelkatz lived through?

As though he read the question on my face he continued:

"And now see, Herr Doktor, do you know an unhappy marriage is an eternity of heartache? And whoever has lived through one is so old—so old—Methuselah is a mere boy compared with him. Nowadays you hear of divorces. In my days they were considered a shame. A divorced woman was regarded as something low, an outcast; and people didn't think very highly either of a man who gave a *Get*. A divorce always had a disgusting flavor. And here in the Khille, once you were mated, there was no way out. Always dragging the yoke, always dragging it along! So believe me God, I really don't want to say anything against Madame Eichelkatz—I am sure she suffered as much from it as I did—but there was no getting away from it, we just didn't suit each other. My simple nature, my straightforwardness, and my lack of education were certainly as obnoxious to her as her culture, her fine manners, and her aristocratic desires were to me. She didn't like my having to stand behind a counter, and I didn't like her speaking French with the Herr Oberstleutnant Von Boddin. Now tell me, Herr Kreisphysikus, do you think it is proper for a *bekovet* Jewish woman to drop curtseys, to laugh loud, and amuse herself with the officers in front of her husband's store when they pass by toward evening? It was 'gnädige Frau' and 'Madame Eichelkatz' and a chattering and laughing and always that 'Madame Eichelkatz.' She refused to see that they were having fun at her expense and made mock of the name Eichelkatz, my good, honest name, Herr Kreisphysikus."

Poor Simon Eichelkatz! So jealousy was his life's woe.

As if endowed with clairvoyance and the ability to read my thoughts, he looked at me sharply and said:

"You must not think that I was jealous, not what one understands by that word. Upon my honor, I was not. When I married my wife, Friederike, *née* Böhm, there was no talk of love between us. We married as all people married then. I had entered Joseph Böhm's business as clerk, and later I married into it, because Böhm could not continue to carry it on alone. He himself came to me and said: 'Simon, if you want to marry my daughter

Friederike, we needn't pay a Shadchen, you needn't and I needn't. You know the business. It's gone backward within the last year; but if you look after it, you will advance it again. You know it once was a good business, and I can no longer keep up against the competition of others; but you can.'

"It flattered my ambition that Herr Joseph Böhm, one of the chief wholesale dealers in Silesia, should offer his daughter to me himself, to me, who only three years before had entered his business as a poor, unknown clerk. Simon Eichelkatz, who was Simon Eichelkatz? Born in Tarnow, of poor, decent folk, I came to Reissnitz and made my fortune there. Just think! The son-in-law of Joseph Böhm! Such a thing had never been! But to become a son-in-law you must have a wife; and I took Friederike Böhm, who was aristocratically brought up, and could speak French."

To-day it particularly struck me what it was that so peculiarly characterized his manner of narrating. As soon as he spoke about personal matters or told stories of the Khille, he fell into the jargon and the intonation of the Jews of former times.[*] But when he dealt with generalities and gave expression to ideas and speculations, his speech acquired a swing, his expressions became almost choice, and the form scarcely ever detracted from the matter. He grew, as it were, beyond his own bounds; and I thought I saw before me not a simple old Jew, but a sage.

[*] The translator has found it impossible to convey this subtle distinction in English. It shows itself in the German by slightly mispronouncing words, for instance, *Leit* instead of *Leute*; using *ä* instead of the article *ein* (an), and very slightly changing the correct order of the words.

"What did they know at that time of such notions? They harnessed two human beings together and said, Now see how you get along with each other." A shadow flitted over his countenance, usually so mild.

"And yet," I interposed, "Jewish marriages as a whole were seldom unfortunate."

"That was because husband and wife were confined to their own homes, their children, and at most to their Mishpocheh. Nothing strange, from the outside, came to disturb them. Life passed in the closest relation of two human beings. Nowadays it's different. But if it happened to be different in my time, it was a calamity—and it was a calamity that Frau Friederike Eichelkatz, *née* Böhm, had learned to speak French. During the first year things went pretty well. To be sure, even then she spoke scornfully of having married an uneducated man, who knew nothing but whether cloths were bad or good, who could tell at the first glance whether a piece of cloth came from Cottbus or from Brünn, whether it was manufactured in

Germany or in England, whether the woof was wool or thread, and whether the wool was pure or mixed. All this was of value in business, but not in marriage. Marriage requires other knowledge to create happiness. And when my wife would ask me so mockingly: 'Do you suppose anyone in Tarnow knows French?' I had enough for a whole week.

"But I always answered back; and that's what made the trouble. I didn't have peace and quiet until I realized that it's best not to say a word, not one word. By the time I found this out it was too late. I believe, Herr Doktor, one always is too old by the time one learns sense. It doesn't do yourself any good any more, and the young folk want to get their own foolish experiences. And so it's really no use to get sensible."

"How can you say anything like that, Herr Eichelkatz? Haven't I the pleasure of listening to so many experiences of yours which interest me and give me food for thought? Don't your stories of the congregation give me a picture which is significant to everyone who loves his people, loves them faithfully and with sorrow at the heart? Besides, wasn't it through the events and incidents of your life that you arrived, whether early or late, at that state of peace and calm which beautifies your old age?"

He listened to me attentively, and a melancholy smile played about his mouth.

"Peace and calm, Herr Kreisphysikus, are to be found only after pain has been gotten rid of in life. But to get rid of pain you must *have* it first. I have had much pain, much pain, and great Tzores; and now when sitting here so quietly, you know—believe me—Herr Kreisphysikus, you by and by become accustomed to that other peace, without end, and you think of it without dread or horror. Sometimes you even—well, we won't speak of it, Herr Doktor. Praised be God for having bestowed such a long life on me. My wife has been dead twenty years and—"

I waited in a state of tense expectation that he would say something about his son; but he hesitated for only an instant and continued:

"We lived together thirty-three years. Do you know what that means, Herr Kreisphysikus, if she looked down on and despised her husband in the very first year of her marriage? Because he wasn't so fine as she, merely an immigrant from Galicia? Because his Mishpocheh were poor people, and his father wasn't a wholesale dealer, but merely a peddler, and because he didn't know French? Even though I showed them later that I knew something and was something, and even though all the others appreciated me, in the eyes of Madame Eichelkatz I always remained a creature of a lower order, an intruder, an upstart. And she never forgave her father for having made me his son-in-law. The better I succeeded in business, and the wealthier we grew, the prouder and more arrogant she became. I was good enough to earn a living, and she had no fault to find with my business career; but as to the trouble I took to cultivate my mind, she paid no attention to that. For her I always remained Simon Eichelkatz from Tarnow, an employee in her father's business, a person with an absurd name and no manners, whom she had married at her father's wish and command. 'How did you happen to marry such a husband?' the Oberstleutnant Von Boddin once asked her, while standing in front of the shop door. 'It's a genuine *mésalliance.*' I was standing behind the counter, and I felt that what the Oberstleutnant was saying was a great insult to me, even though I didn't know the meaning of the word. But I couldn't go and knock him down. Now could I, Herr Kreisphysikus? I, a Jew, and he an Oberstleutnant? But I made a mental note of the word, and I kept repeating it to myself: *mésalliance, mésalliance.* Then, the next Shabbes, after *Mairev,* I went to the Herr Rabbiner and asked him what it meant. When he explained it to me, I all of a sudden became real quiet and thought to myself, why the Herr Oberstleutnant after all is perfectly right. It *was* a *mésalliance.* A failure of a marriage, I tell you, Herr Doktor, and it didn't get any better through the birth of our son in the second year. As long as her father, Joseph Böhm, was alive, she had a little consideration; but after his death that stopped. She sought company of her own. She associated with the Goyim, with the Frau Rechnungsrat and the Frau Kanzleirat, and more such aristocratic *Shnorrers,* who accepted many a little favor here and there from their well-to-do friend. Then came the misfortune with the Oberstleutnant and the officers, who had their sport with the handsome Jewess. She became more and more conceited and foolish; she was ashamed of her husband; and one day she had visiting cards engraved with 'Madame Eichelkatz, *née* Böhm.' The name stuck to her in the Khille. They began to despise her and to pity me."

It had gotten late. I had another professional visit to pay, and I took leave of my old friend. I am looking forward eagerly to his future revelations. As I crossed the Ring past the shops, I suddenly saw, in my mind's eye, an industrious man, humbled by his lot, standing behind the counter, and before the door a handsome woman. And I murmured to myself: "Madame Eichelkatz, *née* Böhm."

OCTOBER 23.

Late this afternoon I hunted up my old friend in the expectation that he would continue the story of his life. Mention had been made of his son, though only *en passant,* and I cherished the secret hope that Simon Eichelkatz would return to him now that he had once begun to pour out his heart to me. But to-day he didn't say anything bearing on what had gone before. When I entered, I found him in a gay mood; and before I crossed the threshold he called out to me:

"It occurred to me to-day that I wanted some time or other to tell you a *Maaseh*, which is half funny, half sad."

And he only recounted anecdotes. Not one word about the events in his life—only the story of the great dearth and famine. Simon Eichelkatz was right; it is a tragi-comic history.

"It was a year of famine after the war of '59; sickness everywhere; bad harvests, bad business; the potatoes rotting in the ground on account of heavy rains and floods. Herr Kreisphysikus, to understand the misery of the people thoroughly, you must live through such a year here.

"All over the mining district typhus, for which the stupid workmen and peasants thought there was only one remedy, the whisky flask. The women and children died miserably on their foul, ill-smelling straw heaps, the men in the ditches. Herr Kreisphysikus, happily it is different now; conditions have improved, it cannot be denied, since forty years ago. Any one might be satisfied to have the difference expressed in money added to his fortune. On that account it's silly always to talk of the good old times. The world's gotten much better, much better. That's what this old man tells you. The winter was terrible that year. To be sure, the typhus grew less severe when the cold set in; but the poor people suffered from the cold instead. Every day you found bodies frozen to death in the ditches by the roadside. Of course they were usually drunkards; nevertheless they were human beings, and such occurrences aroused horror among us. The members of families gathered closer together, they doubly realized the comfort of a heated room and the blessing of a well-ordered existence. Every sign of well-being was regarded with heightened interest; and one day the greatest excitement was caused by the appearance of a new winter coat on the back of the wife of the vice-president. She wore it to Shul for the first time on *Sukkoth*. Frau Wilhelm Weinberger was the wife of a well-to-do man who had brought her the garment from the Leipsic Fair. I can see it now, as though it were yesterday it happened. And you may be sure the other men had it impressed on their memory, too; for you can imagine, Herr Kreisphysikus, it aroused as much envy as excitement; and after Shul most families were probably discussing the coat of Frau Wilhelm Weinberger. It was dark blue, of the finest buckskin, lined with white and light blue striped cloth, and bordered at the bottom with a band of black lambskin. The collar and cuffs were also of lambskin. I tell *you*, Herr Kreisphysikus, it was a marvel."

He chuckled as he always did when something tickled his sense of humor. I did not know whether it was the winter coat of Frau Wilhelm Weinberger which amused him so greatly after the lapse of forty years, or other recollections suggested by it. He paused for a long while before continuing his narrative.

"Besides Teacher Sandberg there were two other teachers in the congregational school at that time, Teacher Deutsch and Teacher Herrnstädt, and two assistants for the lowest classes. All were married and blessed with children; unfortunately, they were not blessed with a corresponding income. The Khille was not in a position to give them sufficient salaries; as it was, its budget for the officers that conducted the services was considerable. So the teachers were extremely hard put to it to support their families in a bekovet way; and in bad times, when it is particularly difficult to get extra jobs, like giving private instruction, they had no smooth road to travel, nebbich. Sandberg had it a little easier, because on his free afternoons he was employed as secretary to the congregation and he kept the minutes of the meetings. But Deutsch had a hard time of it. He had two daughters, and a son who worked in a dry goods store in Breslau. His wife and daughters were very industrious. They did embroidery for the shops, and tried in every possible way to add to the small income of their father. The son also contributed to the support of the family, so that to all outward appearances they seemed to be more than the children of the other teachers. Besides, they always associated with the wealthier families in the congregation. But exactly this was their misfortune. People with daughters were annoyed that the daughters of Teacher Deutsch were always so well-dressed—not like children of a poor teacher, but like those of rich Baale-Batim. The teachers in meeting had decided to ask for a raise of their salaries because of the increased cost of living on account of the famine. They couldn't go on in the old way. The price of bread, potatoes, coffee, and sugar was exorbitant. As it was, they ate meat only once a week, on Shabbes; and it was impossible to obtain the fuel needed during that severe winter. In a very emphatic and touching petition drawn up by Teacher Herrnstädt, the matter was brought to the attention of the president and the board, who were requested to grant an increase to the teachers for the coming year."

At this point Feiwel Silbermann entered with a large cup of coffee and a freshly filled pipe. Simon sipped the hot drink with evident enjoyment, puffed at his pipe several times, and said:

"Yes, at that time things didn't go very well with us, Herr Kreisphysikus. Feiwel, do you still remember the year 1859?"

"Why shouldn't I remember it, Herr Eichelkatz? Am I going to forget how we starved and froze? It wasn't anything, wasn't it? That was a year! The snow lay for four weeks. You wouldn't think there could be such cold, and Teacher Deutsch's daughters got new winter coats."

With this he shambled out of the room and Simon said:

"Yes, the cold was frightful. But in spite of it we were greatly astonished to see Caroline and Lenchen Deutsch, the teacher's daughters, cross the Ring on Christmas day in new winter coats. Of course, we ought to have been glad that the girls had warm clothing in such freezing weather. But human nature is not so indulgent, and the Khille rather bore them a grudge. Everyone ran to the window to make sure of the wonderful fact. 'Look at them,' they called to one another, 'Caroline and Lenchen Deutsch have new coats on. In such bad times! Really, you wouldn't believe it. Chutzpeh!' But the worst of it was that the coats in cut and color, in goods and trimming, were exactly like Frau Wilhelm Weinberger's—blue buckskin and black lambskin—the latest style. The excitement caused by Frau Wilhelm Weinberger's garment wasn't a circumstance to what Caroline and Lenchen Deutsch's called forth. And the consequences, Herr Kreisphysikus, the consequences!" Again he laughed softly. "I don't believe blue buckskin and black lambskin have ever produced such consequences. On the day after Christmas there was a meeting of the committee. The first matter for consideration was the petition of the teachers for a raise in salary. The committee almost unanimously agreed that there was reason in the request. It wasn't fitting that men intrusted with the education of the young should suffer want. In order to have a proper influence upon children teachers should have a free mind and a light heart. Thus spoke Dr. Ehrlich, with great eloquence; and he moved that the petitioners be granted a raise of thirty dollars for the year of famine. Hereupon our honorable friend, Herr Doktor Krakauer, saving your reverence, arose and said he had an addition to make to the proposition: 'to exclude Teacher Deutsch from the benefit of the raise, because for two days his daughters have been flaunting about in winter coats of blue buckskin with black lambskin, coats exactly like the one which Frau Wilhelm Weinberger wears. If anyone can afford that, he needs no raise.'"

A dumbfounded expression probably came on my face, because Simon looked at me, and with that furtive smile of his he said:

"Every word of what I tell you is true, Herr Kreisphysikus. Herr Manasse, *Zichrono livrochoh*, tried to oppose him in vain. He assured the committee that he himself had brought the cloaks with him from Breslau, where the son of Teacher Deutsch, a clerk at Immerwahr's, had given them to him, because he wanted to save the expense of expressing them. They had been lying there ever since the beginning of November, and Teacher Deutsch's son had bought them way below the regular selling-price from a travelling salesman, who had brought them to Breslau as samples months before; one of them in fact was quite damaged. But all that didn't help matters any. Blue buckskin with lambskin remained a crime. It was no use to urge that a good son and brother had pinched himself to give his parents and sisters a pleasure, and that he was able to do it only because the cloaks were cheap and underpriced. Other objections made by two members beside Manasse were also refuted. They say Manasse almost cried when, at the end, he called out: 'But for heaven's sake, they can't eat blue buckskin and black lambskin to satisfy their hunger!' Even that was of no use. Our amiable Dr. Krakauer, saving your reverence, carried his motion, and Teacher Deutsch's petition was refused."

Simon looked into space, then said: "Do you know the real meaning of the word '*nebbich*' Herr Kreisphysikus?"

"Yes, I do, *nebbich*."

OCTOBER 29.

Autumn this year is very disagreeable. It rains a great deal, and the damp, foggy atmosphere has a bad effect on health, both in the city and the country. I have had a great deal to do. Simon Eichelkatz was also indisposed for several days. At his age every disturbance of the physical state is serious. But Feiwel Silbermann is so touchingly attentive that the care he bestows upon the old man quickly carries him through his trouble. My medical instructions are obeyed by Feiwel so punctually and accurately that I can be sure of their effect. We stuck our patient into bed for a few days, but to-day he is sitting up, and this afternoon I allowed him to smoke his pipe. That raised his spirits immediately, and he became more talkative. A light veil of sentimentality still lay on his soul, often the case with convalescents, and he at last returned to the narrative of personal experiences. He remembered a sickness he had had in 1867, late in the summer—a sort of dysentery or *cholera nostras*, then epidemic. "The real illness lasted only a few days, but afterwards," he said, "I was so weak, I couldn't stir a finger. I remember it as though it happened to-day, how I sat before the shop in the sun, to draw some warmth again into my bones. They fairly rattled. I didn't have a Feiwel Silbermann to look after me then."

"And your wife?" I asked.

"My wife wasn't at home. She was in Warmbrunn with our son, who was to recuperate there. He had just passed his final examinations at the Gymnasium. He passed them splendidly, Herr Kreisphysikus. They even excused him from a part of his oral examinations. The whole city spoke of it; and when Herr Professor Lebeck came in the afternoon to buy cloth for a pair of trousers, he said to me: 'You may be proud of your son, Herr Eichelkatz; he does credit to you and to our Gymnasium. It's been a long time since we've had so gifted and industrious a pupil.' Lebeck's red nose glistened as though he had come directly from Heimann to me. Of course, I

- 51 -

sold him the goods very cheap; and as he went out he repeated: 'Yes, your son, he'll be something extra some day.'"

Simon Eichelkatz looked down thoughtfully, then he blew a thick cloud of tobacco smoke into the air and added:

"Fortunately, it passed quickly; only the after-part, until I got back my full strength—but still it wasn't necessary to disturb my wife in her holiday, and my son. At first Herr Doktor Merzbach wanted to write to her; but when I explained to him why I didn't want him to, he gave up the idea. Why? Herr Kreisphysikus! Madame Eichelkatz would probably have come back, if news of my illness had been sent to her; but she wouldn't have brought love into my house, and no good will, and no devotion, just what a weak, sick man needs. On that account I preferred not to have her here, but to let her amuse herself there with her company. It had just then come into style to go away in the summer; and this was the first time Madame Eichelkatz, née Böhm, had followed the fashion. And there she met her good friends. I told this to the Herr Rabbiner, and he thought the matter over and asked: 'Can nothing be done, Eichelkatz, to bring peace into your married life? Now that your son is grown up and ready to go to the university?' I felt as though the Herr Rabbiner were reproaching me. And then for the first and last time I opened out my heart freely. Perhaps because I was so weak and alone. I told him what vexations and humiliations I had endured for twenty years. And always carrying the trouble in secret, so as not to give offense and for the sake of the child. He was not to see how matters stood with us, and besides he was greatly attached to her and loved her tenderly, for she had taken him entirely to herself. I ask you who was Simon Eichelkatz of Tarnow? At most a decent, industrious fellow, who, however, didn't trust himself to say what he thought. It was the custom, you know, in Jewish homes for the women to concern themselves with the house and with the bringing up of the children, and for the men to earn a living. But there was perfect understanding between husband and wife, real harmony; and the mother taught the children that the father, who looked out for them and worked for them, was the centre of the household. This was utterly lacking with Madame and myself. I always remained a stranger to both mother and child. She chose his companions from among the Christians with whom she associated, and she estranged him from Jewish ways exactly as she had estranged him from his father. She kept up the necessary appearances before the outside world; but within our home it looked very bad. The boy was not put on a sure, sound basis for the future. I know it now, Herr Kreisphysikus. Earlier in life I could not see things so clearly. But when Dr. Merzbach came to me that time, I realized all; and I told him everything, even that it was too late to change matters, since my son was almost nineteen years old and would leave home. Dr. Merzbach recognized the truth of what I said, because he didn't say anything in reply. Then I went on and said: 'Believe me, Herr Rabbiner, if two human beings are yoked together and do not go in exactly the same way, hand in hand, but one pulls to the left, the other to the right, they cannot reach a common goal. For that matter they have no common goal.' The Herr Rabbiner shook his head and asked: 'How about your son's future?'

"'Each of us will probably wish for a different future,' I answered. And that's the way it was, Herr Kreisphysikus. What *she* wished came to pass. Her son became a very renowned man. She didn't live to see his greatness, and I who did, I hadn't longed for it."

He paused, as though revolving his words in his mind and added:

"You mustn't misunderstand me, Herr Kreisphysikus. But what has our personal happiness to do with external success? What can one ever receive from others that does not exist in oneself? Hasn't every happiness a different form? Hasn't every happiness a different name? Honor is happiness to one man, wealth to another, beauty to a third, fame to a fourth. Hasn't happiness a thousand names and forms? And have you ever seen two beings who call the same thing happiness? There may be a few things that are looked on as happiness—contentment, health, fulfilment of duty, wealth—but, my dear Herr Kreisphysikus, that only sounds nice—it may be a part, but it is not the whole. That which all men wish to possess is not the happiness that each individual imagines for himself; because it depends upon the nature of each individual; and there are as many happinesses as there have been men since the creation of the world. Or, if you wish it, Herr Kreisphysikus, there is no such thing as happiness at all. Because, if you can't see a thing and say, it is thus and so, does it exist? I can say, this is an apple, this is a potato, this is my pipe; but I can't say, this is happiness. How does it look? Round or long, wide or narrow? I must laugh when I think that Madame Eichelkatz, *née* Böhm, and Simon Eichelkatz should have said, that is our happiness, that's the way it looks, that's the way it should look."

He waved his hand.

"I know all; I know what you want to say, Herr Kreisphysikus, and what Herr Dr. Merzbach also said that time. Our son! Do you know the sort of picture Madame Eichelkatz drew for herself of her son? Great and renowned in the large outside world, so renowned that Herr Oberstleutnant Von Boddin and Frau Steuereinnehmer Antonie Metzner, her bosom friend, would open their eyes in astonishment. That's the way *her* happiness would have looked. She was ambitious and proud and knew French. And do you know how my son looked in my dreams? A good, fine man, an honest Jew, who would conduct my business. I was simple and industrious, and I knew all about cloth. So you may believe me, Herr Kreisphysikus, a Madame who speaks French, and a Jew who can tell at a glance without touching it whether a piece of cloth comes from Cottbus or England, two people like that have very different ideas of happiness!"

I followed his words with increasing astonishment. How do such ideas regarding individuality and such clearly-defined notions of eudæmonism arise in the brain of this old man living remote from the world? Whence this wisdom? While these questions agitated my mind, he continued:

"On that afternoon when I sat in the sun in front of my shop, I began to ponder about these things; and since then I have accustomed myself to reflect about this and that by myself; because I hadn't a single friend with whom I could talk myself out. But, do you know, Herr Doktor, I think it is better to be alone if one wants to think. And Dr. Merzbach passed by and saw me sitting there alone; and, while he was talking to me, Rittmeister Von Blücher and Major Von Schmidt cut diagonally across the Ring to come up to us. Both stepped up and greeted the rabbi, who enjoyed great consideration among the Christians.

"'How do you do, Herr Doktor,' the Rittmeister called out and laughed: 'Do you know the news? To-morrow I shall have the Jew Haberstroh shot; he was delivered up to us from Oswiecin as a spy. He's said to have served in the Austrian army near Neuberun.'

"Dr. Merzbach answered quietly:

"'Since you laugh over it, I'm not worried, Herr Rittmeister. I understand your joke. You would not laugh if a human life were actually at stake. At all events, it's really a sad story that just this good, decent old man should be falsely suspected and delivered up.'

"'Well, what shall we do with the fellow, Herr Doktor? According to military law, he ought to have been dead long ago. Ask the major if I'm not right.'

"'I don't doubt the truth of your words, Herr Rittmeister; but I also know that both you gentlemen would not have a poor innocent man put to death on an unproved accusation. I pledge myself for Haberstroh's innocence.'

"'Tut, tut tut, Herr Doktor, will you be answerable for the consequences?'

"With these words they left the rabbi, laughing, and Haberstroh was not shot to death. After a few days it turned out that he had been arrested on the spiteful charge of a business rival. Dr. Merzbach had gathered the proofs and handed them over to the Rittmeister. He himself had gone to Oswiecin for this purpose. That's the way he always threw himself into affairs, and helped with all his energy."

I was just about to put a question to Simon Eichelkatz about the spy, when he suddenly said:

"Do you believe, Herr Kreisphysikus, that to be good and noble and help your fellow-beings is happiness?"

"Have you ever read anything by Goethe or heard of him?" I returned, evading the question.

"No, Herr Doktor, I never read anything by him, but I've heard of him."

"Goethe says: 'Let man be noble, helpful, and good.' Do you suppose by these words he wanted to show men the road to happiness, Herr Eichelkatz?"

"Who can tell?"

NOVEMBER 11.

A clear winter has at last come after the foggy days of autumn. It has been snowing for several days, and in the morning Jack Frost draws crystal flowers on the window panes.

This morning I received a remarkable epistle from my mother. Its tone is very different from what I am accustomed to in her. As a rule she avoids all interference with my private affairs; and now, all at once, she writes, she doesn't think it proper that I cut myself off, as I do, from all intercourse, and open up no relations whatsoever with the prominent members of the community. She goes on to say that she has learned from trustworthy sources that very fine and cultivated families live in Reissnitz, who would esteem it a pleasure to see me in their homes, and who are probably hurt even now that I do not introduce myself to them. She remarks that I am not intimate even with my colleagues, who would be justified in making a claim upon me. In the house of Sanitätsrat Ehrlich I would surely find the stimulus and the diversion I undoubtedly need after a severe day's work in the practice of my difficult profession. It is always a dubious matter for a bachelor to isolate himself; he develops peculiar ideas and habits, and acquires the manners of a social hermit. Who, she'd like to know, is a certain Simon Eichelkatz, to whom I devote all my spare time? Besides, it is necessary for a physician to marry—in order to inspire confidence, for the sake of appearances. I had hesitated too long; as Kreisphysikus I should have had a wife long ago; why, the very fact of being Kreisphysikus presupposes an age not exactly youthful.

I reflected a moment—she was right for three reasons. My thirty-eight years actually do make me seem old to myself. In fact, I am old; and it now occurs to me all of a sudden that I may have failed to make use of the psychological moment to seek and find my affinity. And if I never marry? Is marriage so unqualifiedly desirable? I thought of Simon Eichelkatz. But how did my mother come to hear of him? I didn't recall having mentioned him in my letters to her. As for the other points on which she touched? Ah! A flash of inspiration! Herr Jonas Goldstücker! There it stood black on white! A very reliable gentleman had approached her in a matter referring to me, calling for discretion, etc., etc. Now, the merits of Fräulein Edith Ehrlich were known in Rawitsch also. I had to laugh; but I determined at all events to interrogate my old friend about the persons in question.

I went to him in the evening. Though he sat near the stove, with a blanket spread over his knees, he still seemed to suffer from the cold. He also seemed tired and not so fresh as a few days before. He responded to my questioning look with:

"It's cold, Herr Kreisphysikus; a bad time for old people. Inside nothing to warm you; outside the cold! It chills you to the marrow!" He rubbed his hands and drew the blanket up. Feiwel Silbermann had stepped in, looked at him anxiously without his noticing it, and then put some more coal in the stove.

"We keep up good fires here in Upper Silesia," said Simon, "but what's the use when you begin to freeze inside?"

There was a touch of melancholy in his voice. I laughed and said:

"Feiwel will heat you inside, too."

Then I ordered hot tea and rum for him at once; and a glass of mulled wine every morning during the cold weather.

I was well aware that this prescription would be of little avail; there are no remedies to counteract such symptoms of old age. But he could be given some relief; and after taking the warm drink he felt more comfortable for the moment.

"It's a remarkable thing, Herr Doktor, that man grows into a block of ice, when his time comes. He doesn't die, but he freezes. Just as outside in nature everything stiffens with the frost when the time comes; and all life dies, because the sun is gone, the great warmth. What curdles in us, is the warm current of life, the blood. No herb grows which can prevent it. Forgive me, Herr Kreisphysikus, for speaking to you so openly. But at my age you don't make beans about things any more, and you think all sorts of thoughts—about life and death. And I've always found you a sensible man, to whom I can say anything at all; and if I now say to you: when the long winter comes upon men, nothing will help them, no doctor, no tea, and no mulled wine, you won't take offense, will you?"

"But spring follows winter," I said more to quiet him than out of conviction. He may have felt this, because he smiled mournfully, and his faded features were suffused with a glorified light—the light that fills us with the awe of the infinite when we stand in the presence of the dead.

"What that spring is which follows the winter of our lives, no man knows. I think it is an eternal winter; and if a new life does blossom out of the grave, it is a fresh beginning, which grows from itself, and does not join on to an end without an end." He gazed meditatively into space. "My idea is," he continued, "that death is the only reality on earth. Life is only a seeming. Life changes at every moment and passes, death never changes and remains forever. Tell me, Herr Kreisphysikus, if men grow old, they live seventy years or a little more, and don't they stay dead a million years? Have you ever heard of anyone's living twice, or being young twice?"

It is not the first time I am called upon to notice the profundity of the old man's observations; but it never fails to surprise me.

"Have you never heard of the immortality of the soul, Herr Eichelkatz?" I asked.

"Soul, Herr Doktor? What is soul? Where is it? In what is it? How does it look? Does it fly out of the body when life is at an end? By the window? By the chimney? Through the keyhole? Has anyone ever seen it? Has someone ever felt it? Sometimes I read in the paper about spirits with whom chosen mortals talk. Do you believe it, Herr Doktor? I don't. Has such a thing ever been proved? They are meshugge or else cheats; it always turns out that way."

I had to laugh at the curt way in which he disposed of spiritualism and all its excrescences.

"Nevertheless, my dear friend," I answered, "there is probably a spiritual after-life which manifests itself in our children and grandchildren—a young spring time of life made fruitful by the impulses of our souls."

He wrapped himself more tightly in his cover. A slight shiver went through his body.

"Herr Kreisphysikus, and how about those who have no children, or those whose children go away from them, or those who do not know their own children?—through no fault of their own. Why should they be worse off than the others? What have they done that they should be extinguished forever, while the others live on forever? I don't believe it. For if I did happen to see in the world a great deal about which I had to ask myself why, still I didn't see anything that had no definite plan and no compelling cause, the good and the bad. The thing might not have pleased me, and it might have seemed bad or false, but it had a law according to which it had to be carried out."

There he was dealing with Kantian abstractions again; the categorical imperative came to him instinctively. I did not want to tire him with thinking too much, and I said:

"By the way, Herr Eichelkatz, I wanted to ask you something that is of personal interest to me. Who is Herr Jonas Goldstücker?"

He looked at me slyly.

"Are you trying to provide for a spiritual after-life, which will manifest itself in your children and grandchildren?" He repeated my words with a touch of irony in the intonation. "And Herr Jonas Goldstücker is to help you on to immortality?"

"We haven't reached that point yet, Herr Eichelkatz," I answered laughing, rejoiced that I had made him think of other things. Without his noticing it, I turned the conversation upon my colleagues in the place, especially Sanitätsrat Ehrlich.

"I don't know the people of to-day very well, Herr Kreisphysikus. Since I gave up my business I haven't bothered myself much about them. The present Sanitätsrat Ehrlich is the son of the Sanitätsrat Ehrlich who was one of the trustees along with Dr. Krakauer. He studied at the same time as my son. And when Ehrlich had finished his course, he established himself here and took up his father's practice. He married and reached a position of prominence and wealth in the same place as his father, who has been dead ten years. If that's what you mean by after-life, Herr Doktor, then the old Sanitätsrat Ehrlich actually does live on in his son. They say the son uses the very same prescriptions as his father. He's not a shining light; but he's a fine, respected man. I believe in time he was made trustee, like his father; and he has children, sons and daughters, who are a satisfaction to him. His oldest son is also studying medicine, and will probably some time take up his father's prescriptions and his practice. The old Sanitätsrat Ehrlich was no shining light, and neither is his son, and I don't know the young one at all—but, at any rate, their light burns a long time, like a *Yom Kippur* light, and in the Khille it may be said of this family: *Ehrlich währt am längsten.*"

He smiled, and was pleased at his own little joke, and I for my part was glad to have left him in a better mood than I had found him.

NOVEMBER 18.

My old friend grows perceptibly weaker. There are no symptoms of a definite trouble but *senectus morbus ipsa*. The nasty cold penetrates the chinks at door and window and settles in some corner of the room, however carefully warmed and provided against weather. The very time of year prepares mischief for an old, decaying body. If Simon were sitting in some sunny spot, who knows if his seventy-eight years would be oppressing him so? What remarkable old people I saw in the south, especially in Rome. They bore their eighty or ninety years with proud dignity and fine carriage. We of the north age much more rapidly; perhaps we are not even born young. Especially we Jews! Conditions have been bettered in the course of time, since our young people have been allowed to benefit by the sanitary, hygienic, and æsthetic achievements of modern life. They all devote themselves to sports, and the obligation to serve in the army has forced them—and the need therefor is highly significant—to practice gymnastic exercises to their advantage. Nevertheless they have something old, thoughtful, worldly-wise in their souls. It is the heritage of the many thousands of years of culture, the culture which has won us renown and singled us out among the nations, but has burdened us also and weighted us down with the over-thoughtfulness born of limitless life-experience. *Naïveté* and an easy mode of existence we have lost through this heritage; and that it manifests itself especially in spiritual matters is praiseworthy, though neither gratifying nor exhilarating. How difficult we are! How dependent upon tradition! What deep roots we have struck in the soil of the past! I believe we drag the chains of our long history more painfully than those put upon us by the other nations. And though these chains are wrought of the gold of fidelity and linked with the pearls of wisdom, they weight us down—they weight us down in a world where we are only tolerated— strangers!

Simon Eichelkatz awakened these thoughts in me. Yesterday he told me a great deal again. Remarkable! It is as though he felt the need to unburden his soul of a few more matters before he sinks into the great, eternal silence. But he doesn't suspect my anxiety in his behalf. He chats on heedlessly into the twilight of the early winter evenings. The twilight makes people communicative and confidential. It is the time of intimate secrets. And at such a time Simon acquainted me with the most solemn experience of his life.

"I do not know, Herr Kreisphysikus, how to tell you—when I found it out, I felt a pain as though a piece of my body were being torn away. It hurt! My, how it hurt! I cried aloud! I made a rent in my coat; I threw myself on the ground, and I sat *Shiveh*. My son was dead, my only child! Madame Eichelkatz said nothing. She remained immovable. Not a sound passed her lips; and to this day I do not know what she thought or felt when the news came that our only child had been—baptized! He had had himself *baptized*, Herr Kreisphysikusleben. Converted! Stepped from one religion into another as lightly as though stepping from the middle of the street over the gutter onto the pavement! From the painful, dusty road to the elegant, smoothly-paved street!

"'What have you to say to this?' I screamed at my wife. But she said nothing. And she raised no objections when after the Shiveh I declared my intention of giving up the business, because, not having a child any more, I did not know for whom to work. She quietly let me do whatever I decided on in my pain and anger. She seemed entirely broken. But no one learned whether from surprise, grief, or repentance. She faded away, and two years after the terrible event she died from no special sickness. 'As a punishment,' the people said, 'of a broken heart'—who knows what goes on in the soul of such a woman!

"I did not know. And that's where I was wrong in the matter. I know it now. And it's a pity, Herr Kreisphysikus, that you never know at the right time. You are never clever, you never understand, you never do the right thing at the right time. It always comes when it's too late."

He paused in his confidences, somewhat hastily uttered, and looked gloomily into space. Then, as though he had suddenly gathered together his inner forces, he added:

"And yet, when I think it over carefully, it's probably not such a pity. It must be so and can't be different, because to err is human. And it's only by way of error that you arrive at knowledge. In man error is life. When he knows everything, more than he likes to know, then comes death."

Error is life, and knowledge is death! The soul of this old man comprehends everything. Philosophers and poets—he never read a line of their works, scarcely a name of theirs reaches his ear, and yet their finest thoughts are crystallized in his observations. And again, for after a little pause he said:

"Death, what is it, Herr Kreisphysikus? Something else that no one knows, surely doesn't know—forgive me, Herr Kreisphysikus, you, too—although you've studied about life and death—and you're a fine, learned man, a serious, learned man—I know, I know. If anyone could have learned about death you certainly would have—but can one learn the eternal riddles of nature? Who knows her secrets? The greatest learning can't penetrate to them. Do me a favor, Herr Kreisphysikus, if there *is* anyone who knows, tell me; I'd be happy to learn one more thing, before I lay myself down and become a dead man, as now I am a live man."

A startling thought flashed through my mind; but before I could answer him, he said, almost hastily:

"I knew it, Herr Kreisphysikus; you can't tell me. Why? Because there's not a soul who could have discovered it—nobody knows what—we don't know anything."

Ignorabimus!

Ay, there's the rub. The thought has given pause to many another besides Simon Eichelkatz!

But now I was determined to give expression to the thought which a moment before had flashed through my mind.

"That's not so easily disposed of as you think, Herr Eichelkatz. We know as little as you say, and yet we know so much! When the inscrutable fails to yield us anything positive, when the exact sciences can tell us no more, then comes the work of hypothesis, of thought."

He looked at me with great, astonished eyes. A light of comprehension spread over his face, although he softly said:

"That's too much for me, Herr Kreisphysikus, what you are saying—I mean the way you say it—I think I can understand your meaning; and as for the exact sciences, I can imagine what that means, I have heard the words before. But the other word, poth—pothe—it can't come from apothecary? What you mean is that when we don't know about something, others come and try to explain it from what they have thought over the matter for themselves."

"That is called philosophy," I said.

"I know the word," he murmured under his breath.

"And the greatest minds of all times have occupied themselves with it."

"And has anything ever come of it?" he said, an ironical smile flitting about the corners of his sunken mouth.

"Why, yes! For if thinking, interpreting, and reasoning did not make the things of this earth clear to us and throw a moral light upon them, there would be only one course left to us; we should be driven to desperation."

He was obviously trying to adjust the meaning of my words in his mind, for it was after a few minutes' pause that he said:

"And you really believe, Herr Kreisphysikus, that it is of some use? Well, I won't argue with you, because I don't understand—but that we should accomplish anything for the general good through morality, I mean, the same sort of morality for many or for all—that—that seems unlikely to me. I've always found that each man has his own morality, just as every Jew has his own *Shulchan Oruch*. And there is nothing too bad or too wicked for one man to do to another but that he can excuse it as being moral. I've experienced it, Herr Kreisphysikus—I"—he paused an instant—"yes, and why shouldn't I tell you? At the time when my only child forsook the faith of his fathers, he wrote me a letter, yes—and he explained the necessity for his taking the step, and in the finest words and thoughts told me how it is the highest morality to be true to yourself—not to what has been handed down to you by others—and how each must find in himself the moral laws of the world—and how each must free himself in order to strive unhampered toward the light. No one should abide by what others have offered him, for to take is—mercy! And the strong man must not kill himself out of compassion and mercy. But my son said of himself, he was strong, and for that reason, he said, he must go his own way pitilessly, and I should forgive him the pain he caused me—he was not one of those who quietly gives a little of himself here and a little there, as is the custom in narrow circles; he was one of the few—one of the magnificently wealthy—a great giver who gives himself to mankind!"

His voice had risen as he conveyed the contents of the letter to me; but then, as though tired out, he added:

"I know every word by heart. I read the letter a thousand times; and, do you know, Herr Kreisphysikus, so that I'd be sure to understand it and read it perfectly, he wrote it in Hebrew letters."

He drew the Bible that always lay on the table closer to himself, took out a piece of paper showing signs of much handling, and gave it to me. It was the letter.

The depths of my soul were stirred.

"What could I do, nebbich, Herr Kreisphysikus? This letter was the only thing I'd ever read of philosophy. Then—yes, after getting it, I sat Shiveh! Because I learned from the letter: 'Be true to yourself.' And I was true to myself in being true to my religion. 'And each must find in himself the moral laws of the world,'—and the moral law of my world is to hold sacred what the God of Israel has commanded. But I hid my sorrow in my soul, and I never again reproached Madame Eichelkatz with having led him into error through her education. What could a frivolous Madame Eichelkatz do, and how could she hinder a man who 'gives himself to mankind,' nebbich?

"She never saw him again, nor did he stand at her grave; because I got the rabbi to write to him he should not come. He answered with only two lines."

Simon reached out again for the book, took a slip of paper out, set his horn-rimmed spectacles on his nose, and read:

"'Weep not, my father! Is not all weeping a lament? And all lamenting an accusation? Accuse not my mother in her grave—accuse not me. Your soul will be healed; for yours is not a petty grief.'

"That was the last I heard from him. Not a tear was shed at Madame Eichelkatz's grave. Then I settled down here with Feiwel Silbermann. I had enough to live on, more than enough, and I began to ponder over mankind and things in general. I've grown old, and I am a stranger to people. Rabbi Dr. Merzbach has been dead a long time, and Cantor Elias, and Meyer Nathanson the Shammes, and Saul Feuerstein, the professional bankrupt, and Dr. Krakauer, saving your reverence, and all the others. The new generation scarcely knows me."

The last words were uttered brokenly, his head sank softly forward. He had dropped off to sleep from sheer exhaustion. After a few minutes he came to himself, and Feiwel Silbermann carried him to bed while I stood there. We administered some bouillon and Tokay wine; but he remained apathetic, and only murmured, almost unintelligibly: "Yes—times change— the Khille is no longer *fromm*." Then he fell asleep again.

I was greatly disturbed on leaving him, and returned the next morning at the very earliest hour possible. He was asleep. Two days later he had passed into the eternal sleep of death.

NOVEMBER 23.

To-day we carried Simon Eichelkatz to his last resting-place. Only a few people accompanied him. But at his grave stood a solitary man.

"Myself I sacrifice to my love, and my neighbor I sacrifice as myself, thus runs the speech of all creators."

The Nietzsche phrase flitted through my mind, a phrase that I had heard explained by the son, the heir of that unlearned, wise old man whom we had just consigned to the earth. "But all creators are hard—thus spoke Zarathustra."

And there—

In a soft though intelligible voice the solitary man repeated the Hebrew words, as he shovelled the earth onto the coffin:

"Dust thou art, to dust returnest; but the spirit returns to God who gave it."

Then he raised himself up, his eye fastened on the growing mound.

Friedrich Eichner!

THE PATRIARCH

Joshua Benas, Geheimrat, arose from his seat at his desk. His smug countenance wore a smile of satisfaction, as he gazed thoughtfully into vacancy, and stroked the close-trimmed beard, already touched with grey.

"Very good," he muttered, with a complacent smile, "first-rate. Elkish has put the matter well. *A la bonheur!* We will declare fourteen per cent dividend; if we strain a point, perhaps fourteen and a half—and enough for a surplus. Great! Splendid!... What a figure we shall cut! No small affair! The gentlemen will be astonished. But after all that is what they're used to; Joshua Benas doesn't fall short of what people expect of him."

He pressed the electric button.

"Tell Mr. Elkish to come up when he leaves the office," he said to the servant who had entered quietly; then he glanced at the clock standing on his desk, a Mercury of light-colored Barbedienne bronze.

"Five o'clock already! Tell Elkish to be here by half-past five."

The servant bowed; as he was leaving the room, his master called after him:

"Is my son at home?"

"No, Herr Geheimrat."

"And my daughter?"

"She and Mlle. Tallieu drove to Professor Jedlitzka's for her music lesson."

"Hm! Very well! Be sure to give my message to Mr. Elkish, Francis."

At this moment an elderly lady of distinguished appearance entered the room.

"Do I disturb you, Joe?"

He dismissed the servant with a nod.

"No, Fanny, if a half-hour will suffice; in half an hour I expect Elkish. At half-past five, Francis."

The servant withdrew as quietly as he had entered, and husband and wife were left alone.

With the eye of the careful housewife she glanced about the room. The luxury of her surroundings had not diminished the traditional concern for minute details of housekeeping. From her mother she had acquired her loving devotion to the affairs of the house. She guarded its growing prosperity, and with a keen eye, as well as a careful hand, she treasured the beautiful and choice possessions with which a fondness for collecting and a feeling for art had enriched her home. Her large corps of servants was capable and well-trained; yet Mrs. Benas would delegate to none the supervision of her household and the inspection of its details.

Her appearance did not betray her habits. She was forty-nine years old; her dark hair, with a touch of grey, was becomingly arranged over a rather high forehead. Her generous mouth, showing well-preserved teeth, and her full double chin gave her countenance a look of energy, softened by the mild and intelligent expression of her eyes. The slight curve of her nose was sufficient to impart to her countenance the unmistakable stamp of her race. But it did not detract from the air of distinction that characterized Frau Geheimrat Benas.

The rapid survey satisfied her that everything was in the best of order in the luxuriously equipped workroom of her husband. Not a particle of dust rested upon the costly bronzes, standing about on desk and mantel, on tables and stands, with designed carelessness. Not too obtrusively, and yet effectively, they revealed the Geheimrat as a patron of the arts, able to surround himself with the choicest works of the most distinguished artists.

Glorious old Flemish tapestries hung above the sofa, forming the background for book-cases filled with the classics of all literatures, and for various *objets d'art*, which a discerning taste had collected. Mrs. Benas's glance rested with particular tenderness upon a few antique pieces of silver, which seemed a curious anachronism in a room furnished in its up-to-date style. They were heirlooms from her parents' home in Rogasen, where her father, Samuel Friedheim—Reb Salme Friedheim as he was called—had been held in high regard. There was the *Kiddush* cup, the *Besomim* box, the *Menorah*, and the large silver *Seder* platter, used by her father; and there were the silver candelabra, the lights of which her mother had "blessed". Her father had been a thrifty dealer in wools, not too greatly blessed with worldly goods; a great Talmudic scholar he had been, however, worthy to marry the great-granddaughter of the celebrated Rabbi Akiba Friedländer, under whom he had studied.

Mrs. Benas's demeanor unconsciously reflected the dignity of such ancestry. She took it as a matter of course that her lot in life should have been cast in the high financial circles, the sphere which gives importance and position to the modern Jew. The son-in-law of Reb Salme Friedheim could not be other than a Geheimrat, unless, continuing the traditions, he had been a student of the Talmud. But, after all, nowadays a Geheimrat is to be preferred to a Jewish scholar or to a modern rabbi; and with pride becoming to her and no offense to her husband she gloried in the aristocracy of her family, without overlooking the advantages her husband's wealth had brought.

The home of her husband had also been in the province of Posen; and it was the respect in which her father had been held throughout the province that had attracted his father, Isidor Benas of Lissa, to the match. Although the dowry was smaller than Benas senior thought he was entitled to demand for his son, the rank of her family weighed so heavily in the balance that Joshua was allowed to court Fanny and win her as his life companion.

His father died shortly after the marriage. Joshua moved the banking and grain business, in which he had been a partner, to Berlin. Here the business prospered to such an extent that the firm of Joshua Benas was soon reckoned among the most influential of the rapidly developing capital. Indeed, it headed all financial and industrial undertakings. Joshua Benas, prominent in the establishment of a large bank, member of the boards of the principal industrial corporations, was appointed Kommerzienrat at the end of the "seventies", and a few years later, in recognition of special services to the Government in the supply of arms, he was made Geheimrat. At the time there were rumors of a high order, which were never made true; and Mrs. Benas gave up the hope she had probably cherished in secret, for the growth of anti-Semitism set a short limit to the honors conferred on Jews, and rendered the dignity of a Geheimer Kommerzienrat the highest to which they dared aspire.

"Credit to whom credit is due," a distinguished professor had equivocally remarked in her drawing-room some years before, in reference to the appointment of a banker distinguished for nothing but his wealth as Geheimer Kommerzienrat. The words ever echoed in her ears. Since then the lesson to remain modestly in the background and be content with the achievements of better times had been well learned. In the meantime, Benas's income had continued to increase; his home grew in splendor and artistic attractiveness, and while his wife watched over the comfort of her establishment and the carefully planned education of the children, she kept pride of ancestry alive in the secret recesses of her soul. The more she felt herself cut off from intercourse with those of her own station in life—the social circle of the elect—the more she cherished the consciousness of her noble descent. The feeling that had been sacred merely as a tradition in the years of social advance, developed in the present days of social isolation—half voluntary and half enforced—into something more intimate and personal. She spoke but seldom of this; all the deeper and keener was the hurt to her pride.

To-day, however, these questions had presented themselves with more insistence than usually. She had received a letter that had led her to seek her husband at this unwonted hour.

As she entered the room a nervous tension was apparent in her features, and, turning to him hastily, after the servant left, she said: "I must speak with you, Joshua, about a matter of great importance."

"Goodness! What's the matter, Fanny? At such an unusual time, and so excited. I hope nothing has occurred. Is it a letter from your sister or...."

During this rapid-fire interrogation she had approached the desk and sunk into an arm-chair.

"Please, Benas, not so many questions at once. I came here to tell you all about it, and I myself hardly know whether this letter is pleasant or unpleasant. It's not from my sister, in fact, from somebody very different."

"Well, from whom? You make me curious. How should I guess from whom?"

"I shall tell you immediately, but please sit down quietly next to me; for we must decide upon the answer."

He glanced at the clock: "I ordered Elkish to come at half-past five."

"Elkish can wait."

"Indeed not! I must consult him about to-morrow's committee meeting of the Magdeburg Machine Construction Company."

"Now, Benas," she interrupted, "there are weightier matters than the Magdeburg Machine Construction...."

"You say that so lightly, Fanny.... I cannot understand how a woman as clever as you are can say such things. The 'Magdeburgs' not important! a small matter! When the balance-sheet is published to-morrow, and the dividends declared, they will rise in value at least fifteen points; and *that*, you say, is of no importance! I must still give my orders about buying and selling; for at the close of the exchange, they will naturally fall, but the day after, then—I tell you, Fanny, it will be a big thing!"

"That's all very good and nice. Money, sadly enough, is the only power we have nowadays; but sometimes other things affect the course of events, as, for instance, this letter."

"Well, what of it? Elkish may come at any moment."

She opened the letter while he turned on the electric light of his reading lamp, whose green silk shade spread a soft, subdued light over the room.

"Regierungsrat Dr. Victor Weilen begs permission to pay his respects this evening at nine o'clock. He apologizes for setting so late an hour, but explains that his duties keep him occupied until late in the day; and inasmuch as the matter which he wishes to discuss is a family affair, he hopes we shall receive him."

"A family affair? He! What does he want of the family? and so unexpectedly! That's really curious. A family affair!"

"He begs, as the time is so short, that an answer be sent to him by telephone, to the Foreign Office, where he will wait until eight o'clock."

"Gracious, how swell! The Foreign Office! And thus do we attain to the honor of telephoning to the Foreign Office," he added satirically.

"What shall the answer be, Joshua? that we are at home?"

"Surely, if you wish to receive him. I cannot understand your excitement, dearest. You have received a Regierungsrat in your drawing-rooms before this, even an Oberregierungsrat. There was a time when Mr. Breitbach found our Moët rather fair...."

"There *was* a time, Benas!"

He frowned. "Well, that's something that cannot be altered, dear child."

At this moment his confidential clerk, Elkish, was announced.

"Even though the 'Magdeburgs' rise ever so high," she answered ironically.

"But that need not hinder you from receiving the Regierungsrat. We're still good for something, I suppose. What think you, Elkish?" he called to him as he entered.

"I do not know to what you refer."

"Well, what else can I refer to but our balance-sheet?"

"As regards that, the firm of Joshua Benas has no need to hide its head," the old clerk responded proudly.

"Well, do you see, dear child?" he said to his wife. "Do as you think best, I rely upon your judgment. You always do the right thing."

She rose. "I will not interrupt you any longer."

"I should like to finish this matter before dinner. There is not much time left."

"Then I shall have Francis telephone that we are at home, and we expect him." She waited at the door.

"Yes, that's all right," he answered, already absorbed in the papers his clerk had spread before him.

"Good-by, Benas! Good-by, Mr. Elkish."

"Good-by, my child," he called to her as she was leaving.

"This only awaits your signature, Mr. Benas. Here. A dividend of fourteen per cent and a half."

"Really, Elkish? I'm delighted!"

"Yes, and here, 240,000 mark in the sinking fund, then 516,000 mark for surplus."

"Excellent! Splendid!" He put on his eyeglasses and signed the various papers placed before him.

"And who do you think will be elected to the board this year?"

"I thought Glücksmann and Ettinger."

"The time for the Breitbachs and Knesebecks is past.... Well, as far as I am concerned, both of them may count upon my vote."

"Mr. Breitbach has not been here for an age," remarked Elkish with a shrewd look.

"Well! To offset that, Herr Regierungsrat Dr. Weilen wishes to visit us to-day—a cousin of my wife."

"He?" The eyes of the old clerk flamed suddenly with burning hatred. "He is baptized, Herr Geheimrat. A grandson of Rabbi Eliezer,.... the first in the family."

"That is not so certain," murmured the Kommerzienrat under his breath.

"And merely to further his prospects! A grandson of Rabbi Eliezer!" Unbounded contempt was expressed by the tone of the faithful clerk, for many years the confidant of his chief, whom he had accompanied from their former home to Berlin.

"How does the cat get across the stream, Elkish? As a Jew he would have had no future, even if he were a direct descendant of King David."

"And is a career everything?"

"One is ambitious, and one must—why not succeed?"

"How about the honorable Geheimrat himself? Haven't you succeeded? If one is able to declare a dividend of fourteen and a half per cent, isn't that success? And if one owns a villa in the Tiergartenstrasse, isn't that what you call success? And if one's son serves with the Dragoons of the Guard? And Miss Rita studies music with Jedlitzka, and literature with Erich Schmidt? She told me so yesterday. Isn't all that success? I tell you, Herr Kommerzienrat, that is success enough. Who buys pictures of Menzel, and busts of Begas, who, indeed? Krupp and Joshua Benas of Lissa. That's what *I* call success." The longer he spoke, the more intense his enthusiasm, and unconsciously he lapsed into the Jewish intonation, which ordinarily did not characterize his speech.

"Not every one can get to be a Kommerzienrat, Elkish. Earning money is unquestionably a very nice thing, but there are idealists who seek advancement in other ways."

"Idealists! Fine idealists, who sell their religion as Dr. Weilen has done. The whole Duchy of Posen was scandalized! A grandson of Rabbi Eliezer! And what does he want of you? Mrs. Benas, I hope, will show him what she thinks of the like of him. I'm certainly surprised that with her views she should consent to receive him."

"He wishes to speak of family affairs."

"Family affairs?" sneered the old man. "Chutzpeh! Perhaps he wants to borrow money of you. That's what usually makes such people remember their family."

"Why, you're in a fine mood to-day, Elkish."

"My mood is always spoilt when I think of such matters, Mr. Benas. After all it is really none of my business. If I had had the *Zechus* to belong to the family of Rabbi Akiba Friedländer, I should not have allowed such a person to cross my threshold."

"Calm yourself, Elkish."

"Why should I calm myself? I am not at all excited. It does not concern me. You must consider what you are doing; and the main thing after all is that to-morrow we declare fourteen and a half per cent."

"Yes, Elkish, after all, that is the main thing."

* * *

At precisely nine o'clock the servant brought in the card of Regierungsrat Dr. Victor Weilen.

As was their custom in the evening when at home to a small circle, the family was assembled in the little round sitting-room. The Geheimrat was seated in an American rocking-chair, near a revolving book-case, in which the evening papers were carefully arranged on their racks. He was smoking a "Henry Clay," and was busily engaged in studying the stock quotations in the "National".

The tea-table, at which Mrs. Benas sat, with its fine silver service, its costly embroidered silk table cover, and with cakes and fruit arranged in beautiful old Meissen bowls, made an attractive picture. An atmosphere of comfort pervaded the room, which despite the luxuriousness of its furnishings made a cozy impression. Artistic vases filled with fresh flowers, fantastically arranged, added to the charm—orchids, delicate and sensitive; chysanthemums of brilliant coloring; bright Chinese lilies curiously shaped, and fire-red berries on thorny branches. Interspersed among these exotic flowers were graceful violets, lilies of the valley, roses, and lilacs, amid tall foliage plants. The display of flowers drew one's attention away from the artistic objects with which the room was filled, but not overburdened. A rich and refined taste was shown in the whole arrangement. Dr. Weilen appreciated it the instant he entered the room. Mr. Benas had advanced a few steps to greet his guest, which he did formally, but cordially, and then presented his wife and his daughter Rita. When the visitor entered, Rita put aside the latest publication by Fontane which she had been reading.

His rapid glance recognized "Stechlin."

Immediately after the entrance of the guest, a young man stepped through the half-open door of the adjoining billiard room.

"My son Hugo," the Geheimrat introduced him. "Referendar at the court of appeals."

"I must again beg your pardon, Mrs. Benas, that I pay my respects to you so late in the evening. But I have something very much at heart, and I did not wish to lose several days only in order to come at a more seasonable hour."

"Let me assure you, in our house the word family affair is a pass-word that overrides conventions, however strictly enforced. In this regard we have carried the traditions of our home into the larger world. The word family always bears a special appeal to us."

He understood quite well that she wished to intimate her appreciation of the obligations demanded by social considerations, which, however, the special circumstances permitted her to waive. With a bow he seated himself near the tea-table, at which the others resumed their places also.

"I am indebted to you for your indulgence. My office hours come at the customary visiting time; and it may have happened that I could not have spoken to you undisturbed, so I took the liberty to claim this privilege."

"Not at all."

In the meantime Rita had prepared the tea, and offered him a cup.

"Thank you."

"Do you prefer a cigar or a cigarette?"

"Is smoking permitted?" he asked of the ladies.

"During the tea hour my wife allows smoking."

"Then may I ask for a cigarette?"

"Hugo, there are the Russian——"

Hesitating, as if overcoming some inner aversion, the young man arose and brought forward a small smoking table with boxes of cigars and cigarettes and smoking appurtenances. Dr. Weilen, with the eye of a connoisseur, noted the wonderful Oriental enamel work in the table. Hugo offered him the cigarettes and a burning wax-taper.

"Thank you, Herr Kollege."

A deep pallor overspread Hugo's face as he bowed silently, while his father said with a smile: "To such dignity we have not yet attained."

"Your son is a lawyer as I am," he graciously said. "I occupied the same position as he does before I was made Regierungsrat. Such is the order of advance. Every one must make a beginning; isn't that so, Herr Kollege? In which department is your work now?"

"In the Exchequer. This is the last year of my preparatory service."

"He has obtained his doctorate, and has served his year with the Dragoons of the Guard," explained his father.

"Then the greatest tasks are over. Would you not enjoy entering the service of the Government?"

"No, sir," he answered in a firm voice. "As a Jew I should have no chances there." The words conveyed an unmistakable insinuation. The sullen fire in his eyes reminded the Kommerzienrat of the appearance of his clerk when he had spoken to him of Dr. Weilen.

The latter appeared not to have heard Hugo's remark, and Mrs. Benas turned to him with some polite phrase, while Rita asked him to allow her to pare some fruit for him.

A harsh, ironic expression lay upon Hugo's face. The moment was ominous, but Dr. Weilen rose to the occasion and said:

"May I tell you now what prompted me to ask for the pleasure of a visit here?"

Mr. and Mrs. Benas looked at him expectantly, and Rita's eyes were fastened upon him with evident interest, while Hugo stared into vacancy, a sombre expression on his face.

"In a few months our uncle, Mr. Leopold Friedländer, will celebrate his ninetieth birthday, on the day before Easter. A short while ago chance threw a Jewish weekly into my hands, in which mention was made of the unusual occasion, and of the significance of Leopold Friedländer's career for Rawitsch. It was not news to me; for at my home mention was often made of my mother's oldest brother, and as a boy I accompanied her once on a visit to him, in order to become acquainted with him. It was shortly after my confirmation,—I mean my—my Bar-Mitzvah. Such childhood recollections remain with one. My mother wished me to recite for him the chapter of the Torah to which I had been 'called up.' This I did, and the impression the moment made must have been very deep, it has remained with me through all the various experiences of my life."

"To be sure," Mrs. Benas felt bound to say, in order to hide the embarrassment which had come upon them. "One never entirely loses the recollections of one's childhood."

"Why should one? They do not represent our worst side. There are occasions in life when they are forced into the background by weightier, more insistent experiences, but they return most vividly in our maturer years at such times when we search our consciences in a confessional mood. When the restlessness of youth subsides, when the struggle for existence is no longer strenuous, when the goal is attained, then it is that the reminiscences of childhood reappear in full vigor. Such reminiscences do not fade, nor become blurred with time."

Rita had regarded him throughout with fixed attention.

"It would be desirable for the shaping of one's career, if such impressions were at all times kept vividly in mind," Hugo said pointedly.

"That is not altogether true," he responded with a smile. "It would interfere with one's development if such influences were ever present. To live amply means to hold control over oneself, and one's personality can be realized and enjoyed only when we have understood and tasted of life in its fulness. Not alone from a one-sided, narrow standpoint, but from the broadest point of view, from the general, the impersonal. Only then can that which is most individual in us develop freely and reach full consciousness."

He relit his cigarette which he had allowed to go out. "But we are wandering off into philosophic byways," he said lightly. "Such is always the case when youth offers us the wisdom of age. You will forgive me, Herr Kollege. It is a challenge to prove one's life not devoid of experiences."

Rita thought her brother had deserved this courteously delivered reproof. What could he have been thinking of when he allowed his unpleasant mood to get the better of him? And toward a guest!

"During these last few days I have begun to realize, with surprise and yet with pleasure, how strongly my past took hold of me. I happen to take up a periodical; my eyes chance to light upon a name, whose sound, long forgotten, re-awakens old memories. In a flash, the old times live within me again. I am deeply impressed—the sensation grows upon me ever more vividly, and at last seeks expression. That brings me to you."

"But how did you happen to come upon this journal?" asked Mr. Benas, merely for the sake of keeping up the conversation.

"At present my interests take me to the department of press and publicity," he rejoined with a smile, "and one finds everything there. That was the way I came upon the notice of the ninetieth birthday of Leopold Friedländer—my—our uncle. The fine old man has attained the age of a veritable patriarch."

"Yes, Uncle Leopold is well-advanced in years," Mrs. Benas added; "the oldest of fourteen brothers and sisters, he is the only one living."

"Is he in good health, and how does he bear his advanced years? I take it for granted you are in direct communication with him."

"Certainly, as head of the family he is highly honored by all of us. We visit him almost every year, and my children, too, have received his blessing. He is vigorous, mentally alert, and reads without spectacles, so that his patriarchal age does not obtrude itself upon his visitors."

"Strangely enough, that is just as I had pictured him to myself. And what of his direct descendants, his sons and daughters?"

"Both daughters are still living, but only one of his three sons."

"Where do they reside?"

"They all married and remained in Rawitsch. Jacob, who is almost seventy years old, carried on his father's business, which is now in the hands of one of his grandsons."

"So the firm is perpetuated from generation to generation. The grandson, no doubt, has a family also?"

"Our cousin is still unmarried."

"And do all live together?"

"Uncle Leopold, since the death of his wife, about twenty years ago, lives with his son."

"My visit to him took place five years before that, when he was still in active business."

"When all the children were provided for, he followed the desire of his heart, and devoted himself to the study of the Torah, a pursuit which, as is natural in the oldest son of Rabbi Eliezer, he had always followed with great devotion. Throughout the whole province, too, he is held in esteem, as if he himself were a rabbi worthy to be the spiritual heir of his famous father."

"These various stages of family life easily escape one moving in quite different circles, but they interest me exceedingly; and I am most grateful to you for this information. The family must have spread greatly, to judge by the number of children our grandfather had; the descendants must be very numerous. Did you know all the brothers and sisters of your mother, Mrs. Benas?"

"I knew all of them, excepting an uncle who died in London, and your own mother."

"She was the youngest of Rabbi Eliezer's children, and died quite young. I, her only child, had not yet reached my fifteenth year. My father married a second time, and consequently the ties of kinship were somewhat loosened, and later, when we moved to South Germany, all connections were broken off. From this time on, I heard almost nothing about my mother's family, and when I left my father's house after my final college examinations, to attend the University of Heidelberg, I was outside the range of all family connections. Shortly after my father died, and as his second marriage was without issue, I was left alone. After the year of mourning, my stepmother went to live with her brother in Milwaukee. She married a city alderman, Dr. Sulzberger, and lives happily there. I give these details, assuming that it might be of some interest to you to learn of the vicissitudes of a near relative, who has come upon you so unexpectedly, even though he is but a branch cut off from the parent stem by peculiar circumstances."

"It is very kind of you to tell us these things, Mr. Weilen. At home, your mother, Aunt Goldine, was often spoken of. And I also heard mention made of the exceptional talents of her son Victor, and of the fact that your father never approached her family after her death."

"I do not know the reasons for this, I merely know the result—an entire estrangement from her family, and that after my father's death I stood quite alone."

"But you might have approached the family."

"Such a step is not natural for a young man who is independent financially—which I was, having become my father's heir—and who believes that he has found a new family in the circle of his fellow-students. I belonged to the most prominent Corps, and became my own master when I came of age. My boyhood, with its recollections of my mother and her circle, seemed a lost world, from which no echo ever reached me. I loved my mother dearly, but at that age it is not considered good form to give in to sentiment; and it seemed to me more manly to suppress my grief. In regard to her family, a certain obstinacy and pride took possession of me. Through all that period there had been no solicitude for me on their part. Why should I force myself upon them? I thought that I had no need of them. Presumably our views of life were wholly opposed. After the death of my mother, my life was spent in very different circles. I confess that even in later years when I went to Posen to visit the grave of my mother, I never thought of calling on the family."

Mr. Weilen's little audience followed his words with mixed feelings. Mr. Benas was eager as to what would be the outcome of his explanations; in Mrs. Benas' family sentiment was awakened; Rita's flushed cheeks testified to the excitement with which she had listened; while Hugo looked sullenly and cynically at the dignified gentleman who spoke so frankly and straightforwardly about himself and the circumstances of his life.

Up to this time the conversation had been carried on chiefly by Mrs. Benas and her cousin. The others listened in silence. But now Mr. Benas interposed.

"Such things," he said, "frequently happen in large and scattered families. It is almost impossible to follow the career of every member. Only those keep in touch with one another whom the peculiar circumstances and conditions of life throw together. My wife has numerous cousins whose names we hardly know, and then, again, there are others with whom we are in constant and close relations. The same is true of my own side of the family. Whoever looks us up and shows a desire to be friendly, is welcome."

"I thank you, Mr. Benas."

"Especially in this case," he continued. "But it is utterly impossible to keep track of every one. Think of it, Dr. Weilen, the father of Rabbi Eliezer, your grandfather and my wife's as well, that is, your great-grandfather, Rabbi Akiba, was married three times, and had nine children.

These in turn married, and no doubt were richly blessed with children, and so on, according to God's commandment: 'Ye shall be numerous as the sands of the sea;' but to pick out all these grains of sand, to observe them, and know them according to their kind, is impossible."

"*I* do not think so, father," said Hugo.

"You seem to be an enthusiastic member of your family."

"I am a Jew."

Dr. Weilen's glance rested with sympathy and interest on the young man.

"But that has nothing to do with our talk, Hugo," said his mother, eager to confine the conversation within safe limits. "Your father merely wished to illustrate how impossible it is to be in close personal relation with all the members of a large, ramified family like ours."

"To which I desire to add the interesting fact," Mr. Benas smilingly said, "that hardly a day passes without the appearance of some one or other who claims to be related to us, either in some remote way through Rabbi Eliezer, or through his father, Rabbi Akiba. Then I always come to the conclusion anew that all Jews are related to one another."

"That they are, father, racially; and they have kept the race pure for thousands of years, and have made it capable of resisting the dangers threatening it from the outside, through fire and sword, and all persecutions and attacks. Only disintegration from within would destroy them—if they cannot put a check upon it—or will not."

"But, Hugo, why always generalize about matters that are of purely personal concern to us? Joe," turning to her husband, "it will surely interest Dr. Weilen, to see to what trouble you went to establish the numerous branchings of our family tree. For our silver wedding, two years ago, my husband had the genealogy of Rabbi Akiba Friedländer's family traced."

"It was not a simple matter," said Mr. Benas, "and the artistic execution hardly cost Professor Zeidler more trouble than the gathering of the data. A young student, also from our home and distantly related, worked almost two years at collecting and arranging the material."

"I should suppose so. And did he succeed in making it quite complete?"

"So far as I can judge, he did succeed. Do you care to see the drawing?"

"Very much."

Rita rose involuntarily.

"Will you show it to Dr. Weilen, my dear?"

"Certainly, mother."

Miss Rita conducted him to her mother's room through the large state parlor, the walls of which, he noted in passing, were covered with canvasses of distinguished artists. In her mother's room, over a small Florentine inlaid table of the sixteenth century, hung the genealogical chart. The room was marked by the same rich style as prevailed elsewhere, but there was something more genial, more home-like in the artistically furnished boudoir. Not a boudoir in the ordinary sense of the word, but rather the apartment of a lady,—luxurious and subtly feminine withal. A soft glow from an iridescent hanging lamp dimly illuminated the room. Rita turned on the electric light inserted in the bowl of an antique lamp, and a bright radiance fell on the large chart occupying almost the entire wall space.

Both stood regarding it without speaking.

Dr. Weilen was lost in contemplation, then he adjusted his eyeglasses as if to see better. "So that is the old pedigree! That's the way it looks! So our tribe has grown and multiplied! How remarkable and interesting!" He was lost in contemplation again, and drew nearer to the chart to study it in detail. It seemed as if he had entirely forgotten Rita's presence; and she remained perfectly quiet, so as not to disturb him.

"Curious," he said, half to himself, "who would have believed it? If I hadn't seen it with my own eyes, I would not have realized the persistent vigor in the old stock." He turned his attention to the right-hand side of the chart, read a few names there, and then said to Rita: "Excuse my abstraction, but it is quite surprising. Are you interested in the history of the family?"

"Of course, I am used to it from childhood up, and my mother has always told me all the peculiarities and incidents of the family."

"And you know your cousins personally?"

"Quite many."

"And what is their station in life?"

"Every possible station. Look at all these branchings and ramifications. There is hardly an occupation that does not claim one or the other. Lawyers, physicians, tutors, merchants,—some very well placed and others less fortunate. One cousin is an African explorer, another has joined a North Pole expedition; and by marriage the women of the family have entered circles as various. Among the cousins by marriage there are architects, professors, dentists, veterinary physicians, engineers, and manufacturers. I think it would hardly be necessary to go outside of the family to find one of every kind, with the exception...." Here she suddenly

- 79 -

paused in her vivacious explanations and stared at him with embarrassment in her large eyes.

"Well, Miss Rita, what branch is lacking on the golden tree of life?"

A vivid blush suffused her face, which appeared all the prettier to him in its embarrassed shyness.

"I will tell you. Do you see here to the right?" and he pointed out the place with his finger. "Here is the name Goldine, the last of the fourteen branches issuing from Rabbi Eliezer, joined to that of Herman Weilen—my parents; and here the broken branch, quite symbolic, do you see?—without a name,—that refers to me."

Anxious fear took possession of her.

"Oh, Herr Regierungsrat," she stammered.

"That's just it—Regierungsrat! I have been deprived of the cousinship on this genealogical tree. A scion without a name, disinherited!"

There was more sorrow than bitterness in his voice, and this gave her the courage to say: "It surely happened unintentionally. Nothing was known of you in our family, and it was taken for granted that you had broken off connection with it. We had only heard...." Suddenly she hesitated.

"Your reasons are significant, Miss Rita, the broken-off branch dares not call you cousin." A peculiar smile played about his lips. "But I should like to finish the thought you would not express. You had only heard that I had discarded the belief of my fathers, had changed my religion, had entered the service of the Government, had made a career for myself, and hoped to reach a still higher goal. That's it, is it not? A broken-off branch, but not a withered one!"

She gazed at him with large, astonished eyes into which a dreamy expression gradually crept.

"To be sure," he continued, "I have no right to complain."

"I never heard any one speak of you in that way," she declared, trying to regain her self-possession. "In fact you were never spoken of;" then, trying to improve the thoughtless expression, "at least not often. I think you are wrong in your judgment, and also in regard to the family tree. I am sure the omission is accidental."

"You are very kind, Miss Rita, you wish to console me. It doubtless seems cruel to you that a man in the full vigor of life, with energy and ambition to reach yet higher rungs on the ladder of success, should be summarily hewn from the parent stem. If I were superstitious, I should fear for my life, for my future. Fortunately I am not, or rather I may be superstitious in believing that side by side with the ill omen there is a good one, in the shape of a friendly young lady; and if she will graciously accept me as a cousin, then the sinister mark on the pedigree will be cancelled. You surely have not forgotten the stories of the bad and the good fairies, because it cannot be so long ago since you were devoted to them. You remember? In compensation for the evil charms of the one, they gave the poor victim the blessings of the other for protection. And I should like to regard you as my good fairy."

There was something very winning, very lovable in his manner and his words, and she answered simply: "You will not need such protection, Dr. Weilen."

"Please, say 'cousin.'"

There was a moment of hesitation, then she said: "You will not need such protection, cousin."

"But I may surely count upon you, should I happen to need it?"

"You certainly may."

Then they returned to the tea-table, Rita somewhat embarrassed, he in high, good humor. "The family tree is exceedingly interesting, Mr. Benas," he said. "You will permit me, I hope, to study it in all its details. Even a cursory glance impressed me tremendously. At the very root, generations back, where there are names testifying to a strong and hardy stock, is the father of Rabbi Eliezer, Rabbi Akiba, a luminary in Talmudic lore, a great man even in those days. Then again, among his children, one excelled in strong individuality and great knowledge, Rabbi Eliezer, and from him and his descendants a numerous progeny, among whom again Leopold Friedländer stands out conspicuous; and so the family tree continues to spread its limbs, luxuriant in leaf and blossom."

Rita hung on his words; she was nervous, fearing a reference to the broken branch. But he said nothing, only fixed his glance on her meaningly. She drew a long breath of relief.

"It was, indeed, a pleasure to me to see the work executed," Mr. Benas remarked, "and my wife received it with great enthusiasm."

"I should suppose so."

They felt their guest was sincere in all he said, and yet they could not rid themselves of a feeling of estrangement. He had introduced himself to them in so peculiar a manner. This equivocal position of close kinship and complete alienation produced a certain constraint, which despite the polished ease and courtesy of the man of the world could not be overcome. And all the time each one asked himself the true purpose of his visit.

As if conscious of the unspoken question, he said: "As is natural when members of the same family meet each other for the first time, we quickly dropped into the discussion of common interests; and in passing from one subject to another, I have not reached the point of telling you what induced me to visit you."

He reflected a moment as if searching for the proper phrase.

"When I read the notice of the anniversary celebration of Leopold Friedländer, I was suddenly overcome with the wish to take part in it. The wish came like a secret longing for—for my home! My boyhood came back to me. I saw my uncle before me as I had seen him then. The years of estrangement disappeared from my mental vision; I heard his tender, hesitating voice again, I felt his hand upon my head, extended in blessing; and I became conscious of the words of the benediction spoken in the language of the race. All that had happened between, I seemed to have forgotten; and it took an appreciable time before I was recalled to myself. But the wish once aroused in me was not to be eradicated, and, ever since, my thoughts have dwelt upon the possibility of its fulfilment."

A peculiar tensity of feeling came over the small circle. They followed his words with growing astonishment; and neither he nor the others thought of throwing off the mood his words had inspired.

"It was quite clear to me that without some preliminary ceremony I dare not intrude upon the family group gathered about him on this anniversary day. According to the traditions of our family, I had forfeited the right; and yet I hoped I might find some appreciation of my position among the younger generation and the intercession I need. I had often heard of your family, Mr. Benas, and I saw your name at the head of the lists of all charitable and public enterprises; and although I was surprised never to meet you and your family on occasions at which common interests might have thrown us together in certain social circles, to which you really belong...."

"Of late years we have withdrawn from all intercourse, except with our own family, and a few intimate friends," interrupted Mrs. Benas.

"But your position involves certain social obligations."

"Nowadays one hardly notices it, perhaps does not care to notice it, if these obligations are not fulfilled," Mr. Benas rejoined with a slightly ironical, slightly pained expression. "Formerly ours were the most successful, the most elegant, and the most entertaining functions. My wife had a gift for entertaining; and it was always a pleasure for us to welcome happy, clever, representative, gay people. Now we confine ourselves to a few formal and official dinners, made necessary by my connection with the leading financial circles."

"We have become used to it, and do not miss anything," added Mrs. Benas. "The spacious rooms which formerly resounded with merry society are now quiet. But a more intimate, a more sincere life has taken its place. Personally I should not feel the difference; but at times I am sorry that our daughter is not able to enjoy the stimulus and the attractions of such social gatherings. In the old days she had not yet made her *début*."

"But, mother, I have often told you that I have no longings in that direction. Your goodness to me enriches my life sufficiently. Whatever is beautiful, great, important, I enjoy."

"But it was entirely different when the people who offered the great and the beautiful things of which you speak came and went freely in our house, in a certain sense belonged to us, were our guests. The foremost artists and men of science used to come here."

"I think, father, it is much pleasanter to know the works than the authors," Hugo interrupted brusquely. "Every one knows what such as they seek in the homes of rich Jews; and when you pay for their services and creations, and ask nothing of them socially, then you do them and yourself the greatest favor."

"That has not always been the case, Hugo. Your views are too severe and rigid."

"It has always been so; only perhaps there were times when it was not so evident. What do we want with their well-meant intentions and condescensions, their forbearances and tolerations, their humanitarian impulses! At bottom it has always been the same. The Jew was always burned!—in Sultan Saladin's time, as well as now. Only now we do not complacently accept such treatment, wagging our tails in gratitude like a dog."

A dull fire burned in his eyes. His face wore an expression of pride and energy.

"I'm afraid, Hugo," his mother said, trying to calm him, "that our guest has but little interest in your opinions. You know, too, that we do not agree with you altogether."

"Forgive me, Dr. Weilen," he said, turning to their guest with the conventional manner and incisiveness of a Prussian functionary and a volunteer of the Guards. "I was carried away by the subject, and then I thought that here at my father's table.... you see, we are not accustomed, nowadays, to have any one with us who does not understand our pain and indignation."

"Nor is that the case on this occasion—at least not since this evening, not since this hour which I have been permitted to spend among you."

Hugo bowed in silence.

Dr. Weilen arose, saying:

"But I must not encroach upon your hospitality too long. You know now what it is I wish. Do you believe a way can be found for me to be present in Rawitsch at Uncle Leopold's birthday celebration? Will the family receive me for that day? Will he himself be disposed to receive me? I beg of you to help me realize this desire of mine. In affairs like this, in which a sympathetic temperament is of more avail than cold reason, a clever and noble woman is the best messenger; and women are fine diplomats, too. May I count upon you, Mrs. Benas, honored cousin?"

"I will consider. But how? As regards the matter itself, I am entirely on your side. But you understand that in a large family there are scores of considerations and prejudices that must be taken into account."

"I understand that perfectly."

"But there is still plenty of time before the birthday celebration."

"Diplomatic undertakings must be arranged long in advance," he laughed.

"I will make use of your suggestion and start negotiations," she said, cleverly responding to his pleasantry.

"And will you allow me to come again, to assure myself of the progress of the negotiations, and to encourage them by my personal intervention? I must tell you that I have felt very much at home with you, not at all like a stranger."

"I thank you, Dr. Weilen," answered his host, politely; and his wife added, "You will always find a welcome here." Thereupon he took his leave, Hugo escorting him to the hall, where the servant helped him on with his heavy fur coat.

* * *

When Dr. Weilen stepped out into the street, gusts of wind blew the snow-flakes whirling about merrily against his face. Tiny, pointed snow-crystals caught in his beard and blinded his eyes. He pulled up his fur collar more snugly, and hailed a passing cab.

He hesitated a moment before giving directions.

He was not in the mood to return at once to his own house; he drew out his watch and saw by the light of the carriage lamp that it was nearly eleven o'clock.

"How quickly the time passed," he mused. "I may still find some of my friends at the 'Hermitage' or at the 'Kaiserhof.'" But as he was about to enter the cab, he decided that he did not care for companionship, and he concluded to go directly to his house, which was in the upper part of Wilhelmsstrasse. On reaching his room, he lit the lamp on his desk, intending to work a little while. But a moment later he tossed his pen aside; he was too restless, and not in the proper mood. He paced up and down the room to regain his composure.

"Remarkable! What refinement, dignity, and self-respect; and not a bit purse-proud or arrogant," he said softly to himself. "The old man—well, perhaps just a wee bit, but even he is very restrained; one can hardly notice it. And his wife, my cousin, quite *comme il faut*,—so ladylike! Why not? The Friedländers are of ancient aristocracy! The mother's blood seethes in the son's veins! Poor fellow! What experiences and sufferings a young Prussian law-student and volunteer of the Guards must have met with to have become so curt and repelling. And this despite the princely fortune which might have flung every door open to him, especially of those houses which a man of his age most desires to enter. Instead of that, half-martyr, half-hero, he fashions his own ideals. An interesting fellow! Evidently talented and possessing the courage of his convictions. How determined he was to vent his opinions, somewhat aggressively, of course, to show me that I did not overawe him in the least. A nice sort of chap! And then little Rita! How modest and quiet, and clever withal, for you could see that she was interested in the conversation, even when she was silent. Her eyes spoke, and so did her mobile little face. And she takes all this wealth quite as a matter of fact; she is to the manner born; she does not regard it as anything extraordinary. Altogether charming!"

He had conquered his restlessness a little during these reflections; he lit a cigar and went over to a table by the fire-place, heaped with books, pamphlets, and journals. A low fire flickered on the hearth. He fanned it to a bright flame, then moved the lamp from his desk to the table and settled himself in an arm-chair.

"I wonder whether they *will* restore me to their good graces! Not only the Benases, but the others,—Uncle Leopold's family. If only for the one day! How I hope they will! I'm actually homesick for—for the Ghetto!"

He took up a book. "If they were to see you now, Victor, the gentlemen of the Foreign Office! Yet a Ghetto it remains for all their liberty and all their magnificence. Whether in the grand drawing-room of the Tiergarten villa, or at Uncle Leopold's in Rawitsch.... That's exactly what the young son recognizes in his vigor and in his consciousness of injured pride. The older ones have become resigned to it."

* * *

In the family of Geheimrat Benas the visit of Dr. Weilen had caused dissension. The father wished to invite Dr. Weilen to dinner in the near future. It seemed to him a matter of course that a guest who had approached them so graciously and unconstrainedly should receive equal courtesy at their hands. His wife was inclined to second him in this view, but she was strongly influenced by Hugo, who decidedly opposed fostering a connection which, experience taught them, might result in nothing but mortification and neglect. At first Rita was a silent member of these councils, but at length she said: "I cannot understand why you talk yourself into such ideas, Hugo. We have no right to be discourteous to a guest who has approached us so politely. Impoliteness is lack of refinement in all circumstances. We do not interfere with your opinions, and therefore you have no right to ask us to have none of our own. But above all, you should not ask us to disregard all the social consideration to which any visitor at our house is entitled."

"Yes, any one except Dr. Weilen."

"But why? You're indulging in pure caprice! Has he done anything or neglected to do anything to cause such brusque treatment?"

Hugo frowned.

"Did he not please you, Hugo?" his mother asked, in a pacific tone.

"Please me? I don't think we have a right to be influenced by our personal sympathies or antipathies. Dr. Weilen pleased me well enough, but he is our enemy, just as every one else.... or rather more than any one else! And therefore I find it unnecessary to give him encouragement. I should not like him to think we are running after him, or feel honored because he condescended...."

"Goodness gracious, Hugo, sometimes you are quite unbearable! If people heard you, they would think you're Elkish. One can excuse such prejudices in an old, uneducated man; but in a modern young fellow of your education they are hardly to be condoned. We do not oppose your ideas and your convictions, but you ought not to go so far as to impose them upon the family! As a result of circumstances beyond our control we find

- 86 -

ourselves outsiders in society; yet we need not carry our resentment to the extent of repulsing a gentleman who has been so pleasant and respectful in his advances. And that only because he is a man in an exalted position."

Mr. Benas spoke with irritation. He continued impatiently:

"Entirely of his own accord he told us how he had happened to become estranged from his family; and no doubt he could explain his further actions. But after all it is none of our business. The sincerity of his manner, his personality attracted me. Of course, at moments we were constrained and uncomfortable, but that was surely due to us, not to him, and above all to your own brusqueness; and his manner of ignoring that was more than amiable."

"We must thank him for this condescension most humbly."

"Hugo!" He met a look of warning and beseeching in his mother's eyes.

"Well, enough of this. We'll invite Dr. Weilen to dine with us next Sunday. It is not to be a formal invitation. Fanny, you yourself write a few lines, and don't invite many people. Ten or twelve will do. In the small dining-room—a simple but elegant affair. However, you're well posted in all those fine distinctions, my lady," he added playfully, to temper the impression of his severity toward Hugo. "And see to it that our young man acquires more normal ideas. I know you are confederates, and secretly you harbor his views."

"Joshua!"

He laughed. "There, you see, I am right. Usually you call me Joe, but in uncommonly solemn moments it is Joshua! Dr. Weilen made the advances, we must invite him, unless we intend to insult him with a repulse, and as we do not want to insult him, we must follow the conventions. I expect you to take this as your rule of behavior toward the Regierungsrat, Hugo. I have no fondness for ostentation or inconsiderateness. Our opinions in order to be sincere and effective need not take the form of aloofness and discourtesy. Remember that!"

The young man looked almost pained; but he did not respond. As he was a Jewish young man, respect for paternal authority was deep-rooted in his being. Moreover, his father was ordinarily so amiable, kind, and considerate toward his children, that when once he was decided and firm, there was no thought of opposing him.

Rita's eyes gleamed on her father. A genial, tacit understanding existed between the two, which leagued them, as it were, against the mother and Hugo. This pretty, good-natured party difference gave a peculiar charm to the intimacy of their family life.

"It is lucky that Rita is my confederate," he laughingly said as he arose, "else, by this time, the shield of David would be emblazoned over the door, and no stranger would be allowed to cross the threshold. In fact, Elkish advocated some such thing when we spoke of Dr. Weilen's visit. Elkish and you on the same platform! For heaven's sake, children, do not let us be ridiculous! I surely appreciate the old man; and during the past days he has brilliantly demonstrated his value in the matter of the 'Magdeburgs,' but everything must be kept within bounds. It is time for me to go to my office now. Fanny, whom do you want to invite?"

"How would Professor Zeidler do—and Jedlitzka, and Hoffman, the sculptor?"

"All right! But no; they have not been invited for some time; and they mustn't think we waited until we could have a Regierungsrat to meet them,—oh, no!"

A smile of triumph flitted about the corners of Hugo's mouth.

"Invite a few of our own family. Justizrat Friedheim, Robert Freudenthal, the architect, and Amtsgerichtsrat Lesser, with their wives. That makes six; we are four; with Dr. Weilen eleven. We need a bachelor."

"Dr. Rosenfeld?"

He laughed. "Well, yes! So that you and Hugo may have support. But now I must go. There's just time to catch Bamberger before the Exchange opens. Good-by, children. Don't get up from the table—*Mahlzeit!*"

Unanimity of opinion did not prevail among the three he left at their breakfast. Nevertheless, before the day was over, Dr. Weilen received an invitation to dine with the Benases on the following Sunday.

On the whole, the dinner passed off very pleasantly. Dr. Weilen, with the ease of the man of the world, made himself at home in the small circle. It was not difficult for him to find points of contact with these men holding a high position in society; and the women were so well-mannered, cultured, and genial, that he quickly lost the feeling of strangeness. Besides, his own being radiated an atmosphere of cordiality, which smoothed over the awkwardness of a first meeting. The greetings between him and his hosts might almost have been called cordial, as between people conscious of spiritual kinship. The Geheimrat was in an especially good humor; and Rita felt inclined to be all the more friendly as she was very apprehensive of Hugo's conduct toward their guest.

Her fears proved groundless. Hugo was too well-bred to act discourteously toward his father's guest. His behavior, though reserved, was faultlessly polite. The appearance of Dr. Weilen, the Regierungsrat, in his home was a *fait accompli*, to be accepted; consequently Dr. Weilen soon felt at his ease in this company. The family connection between him and certain of the guests was not spoken of. No one displayed any curiosity. They seemed to be united by a secret bond. In the course of the dinner the feeling of good-will increased. Dr. Weilen was charmed with the elegant mode of life, and was particularly pleased to see that the forms of good society seemed to come natural to them. Nothing betrayed that they had grown up in different circumstances, and that their present luxury had not been inherited from generation to generation, but had been acquired within measurable time. They had all the manners and accessories of their station. The liveried servants, the beautiful porcelain, the costly silver, the exquisite wines, and the choice dishes were as much in place here as in the most aristocratic circles that Dr. Weilen frequented. The splendor of the surroundings pleased him, not for the sake of the wealth itself, but for the air with which it was carried off. He felt himself attracted to them, he felt a spiritual kinship.

He became especially interested in Justizrat Friedheim, a cousin of Mrs. Benas's on her father's side. He was a man with a powerful, distinguished head set upon a small, thick-set body. Well known in the legal world through his commentary upon commercial law, he had taken a prominent part in behalf of the national liberal party during a recent session of the Reichstag. He had declined re-election on the ground of poor health. However, anyone who looked at this vigorous man, still in the prime of his manhood, would readily surmise that there were other, deeper-lying reasons, not openly mentioned, that deprived the fatherland of the services of this active and distinguished statesman. To his left sat the hostess, whom Dr. Weilen had taken down to dinner, and upon his other side sat Mrs. Lesser. She was a beautiful blonde, with fine teeth, and animated countenance, and lively manners. She was complaining to her neighbor that it had become an impossibility to get into the Reichstag, since he was no longer a member.

"I'm not good for anything any more," he answered, "but all you need to do is apply at the office."

"That's such a nuisance. Formerly it was so pleasant to sit in the members' box, and listen to Bebel and Eugen Richter." With an affectation of alarm she glanced at Dr. Weilen. "I beg your pardon, Herr Regierungsrat."

"The Government is accustomed to evils," jestingly interposed Mr. Friedheim.

She hesitated to reply only one instant; then quick-wittedly: "So we are in the same boat as the Government!"

"We could wish for no pleasanter companions in our misery," Dr. Weilen gallantly said, and raised his glass to touch hers.

It was inevitable that every now and then the conversation should take a dangerous turn, no matter how careful they were to confine the talk to literary and art topics, and avoid politics. But in a circle of intellectual men this was difficult; and the women of this circle seemed as conversant with the questions of the day as the men. However, with perfect tact and good taste, they avoided whatever might have provoked an argument; and though their opinions were expressed with wit and understanding, nothing occurred to give offense. They left the table in high spirits. The temperament of their race came out very distinctly, no less in the case of the Regierungsrat than of the others.

Friedheim, Lesser, and Weilen were chatting together in the smoking-room over their coffee; the host and Freudenthal, the architect, were looking over the plans for a villa on the Wannsee, which had been offered to Mr. Benas. The ladies and the two younger men had withdrawn to the music-room; and presently the strains of Wagner's "Feuerzauber" were heard, played with masterly skill.

"Who plays so wonderfully?" asked Dr. Weilen.

"Mrs. Freudenthal, a famous artist before my cousin married her. Perhaps you heard of her under her stage name, Flora Bensheimer."

"O, of course, the great pianiste?" he asked with interest. "And is she the wife of the architect? Has she given up her career?"

"She plays only for her immediate family. When our cousin married her ten years ago, she continued to perform now and then in public for charitable purposes; but for the last few years, she has given that up as well."

"But that is a loss both to charity and to the public."

"Freudenthal doesn't let charity suffer on that account," answered Mr. Friedheim. "He is very rich and gives generously on all sides; but he holds that he has no further obligations to the public. The remarkable talent of his wife he keeps from the world ever since it was subjected to affront. He can dispense his money without attracting notice; but he must conceal his wife's art so as not to attract undue notice."

"But that is egotistical."

"Perhaps. He is peculiar. The marriage is a childless one, and his wife is everything to him, wife and child in one."

"And was it easy for her to decide to give up the fascinations of a public career? She is known all over the world."

"Freudenthal has transplanted her to the best of all worlds, to the shelter of a loving and devoted marriage. He idolizes her and casts laurel wreaths and diamonds at her feet, such as have never been showered upon any other artist—a whole grove of laurels around her villa at Nice, and as for the diamonds—consult the ladies about them; they know about such things."

Dr. Weilen was amused by Mr. Friedheim's sarcastic manner, and he rejoined: "I should like to hear about them. At all events I shall look up the ladies."

The closing chords of the "Feuerzauber" died away, as he arose quietly and went to the adjoining room. He had observed Rita through the open door.

She was listening to the music, lost in revery, and she started with surprise, when she suddenly heard at her side: "Are you musical, too, Miss Rita?"

"Yes, a little. In our family we all play. Music is so inspiring, and we seem to have a talent for it. I do not mean Flora Freudenthal, who has married into the family, but there is Mrs. Lesser, a cousin of my mother and of Mr. Friedheim, herself a Friedheim, who has a superb voice. She was trained under the most distinguished singing masters; and some of my other cousins have a fine understanding of music, and devote much time to it."

"I suspect it is a Friedheim gift; for I myself am not at all musical."

She reflected a moment before saying: "It seems so, Dr. Weilen, though I never thought of it before. Those on the Friedländer side have other talents."

He smiled. "You are very kind."

Slightly embarrassed, she answered: "That was not an empty compliment. My mother's relatives on the maternal side have done much in scientific ways. Professor Jacob Friedländer in Breslau, Professor Emil Friedländer in Marburg, Professor Felix Friedländer of the Karlsruhe Polytechnic, are all men of scientific note; as is also Professor Ernest Biedermann, whose mother was a Friedländer, and who is a leader among modern German painters."

All unconscious though she was of it, her words reflected pride and joyous enthusiasm. A slight flush overspread her face; her animated glance rested involuntarily upon the family pedigree that hung opposite to them.

"You are well acquainted with the positions your relatives occupy. Do you visit them?"

She was startled at his words as though she had discovered a false note in them, irony and derision. But he looked at her so innocently and so sympathetically that she was ashamed of her mistrust.

"Not at all. Occasionally we meet Professor Biedermann. As a rule his calling takes him into quite different circles."

"And who are the people who would not be glad to have the *entrée* in such a home as your parents'?" he asked thoughtfully.

"My parents have not cared for a wide circle of acquaintances for years. My father, whose eminently successful career and public services entitle him to a certain amount of pride, scorns to be put in a position where he is merely tolerated; and my mother's pride is no more able to bear rebuffs." She paused in alarm at what she had said. Why had she allowed herself to be so carried away? She had been overcome by the everlasting woe and sorrow of her race, which arise anew in every generation; and this in the presence of a stranger,—of this stranger.

She looked at him timidly, with a troubled expression.

"Why do you not continue, Miss Rita,—or may I call you cousin, as I did before? You have no idea how much I am interested by what you say. I have met Professor Biedermann, but I did not introduce myself as cousin."

"Indeed!" she answered suddenly becoming quite cold.

"Do not misunderstand me. You see, all these cousins of whom you spoke have very plainly given me to understand that they have renounced me; for otherwise one or the other of them who moves in the same walks that I do would some time have bethought himself of me."

"How could you expect that?" she said eagerly. "You are unjust. You were the one to withdraw entirely from the connection, without possibility of recall." Again she hesitated.

"Do you believe that unprejudiced men would lay that up against me?"

"I do not believe that exactly; but what cause would there be for them to approach you? Those who have need of the family can always find a place in it, and there are many such, alas, many, far more than those who have attained a position in life. The family connection establishes a common interest; and this keeps them in touch with one another permanently. At family gatherings every now and then one hears of some good fortune that has befallen one or the other, and this brings pleasure to each member of the family. My mother especially is very well informed, and is anxious to learn of anyone who has risen to importance or honor. And now we speak of an event of that kind oftener than formerly; we take it as a consolation, a comfort, that one of us has attained to some position, even though it be only what was well deserved, without...."

"Say it openly, without baptism."

A deep flush covered her face, and in her eyes there were restrained tears.

To what had the conversation led her? To a point at which he could not but be hurt. She looked at him helplessly, unable to utter a word. At length she stammered, "O no, that—I—that was not intended—I...."

"Why should they not say it? In reality, it is not an easy matter for those gentlemen to attain the positions that are their due; and therefore their promotion is received with especial delight, not only by the family, but by the congregation, by the whole race. And now at last I hear the tale from a wholly fair and unprejudiced source."

She gazed at him with open doubt.

"Aren't you unprejudiced, Miss Rita?"

"Not any longer," she answered, with a sigh. At this moment her mother entered.

"Rita, Betty is going to sing, won't you accompany her?"

She arose quickly, as though released from some dread oppression.

"Gladly, mother."

He looked at her with a quiet smile. She noticed it, and was again overcome by her shyness. What must he think of her? Like a babbling, foolish child, she had inconsiderately touched upon subjects bound to lead to painful discussions,—topics that all had tactfully avoided, all except herself, the last person to intend an insult. If Hugo had said such a thing, how it would have irritated her, and in his case it might have been excusable; but she—was it fate, a spell that forced her thoughts in such directions? It seemed as though these questions cast a shadow over her every thought and action. That an innocent conversation should suddenly and involuntarily take a turn that gives an equivocal meaning to everything said, should give her words unintended innuendo and insinuations— nothing was farther from her thoughts; and yet the thing had occurred. It was only the interruption of her mother that had saved her from further indiscretions.

"Our cousin Betty, Mrs. Lesser, has a charming voice."

"So Miss Rita has just told me."

"So, Rita, you have been entertaining our guest with the recital of the talents of our family?"

"She has done so, excellently; I have the liveliest interest in them, and am truly grateful to your daughter."

He looked at Rita with a lingering glance. She returned it. Their eyes met, and then she bowed silently and went into the music-room. Presently Schubert's "Wanderer," was heard, beautifully rendered.

"And ever longing asketh where!" was the sad, melancholy refrain. "Ever where!"

He shook his head as if to rid himself of a sad thought.

*　*　*

Dr. Weilen took leave, promising to come soon again. Both Mr. and Mrs. Benas had invited him to repeat his call. The other guests, who had gathered in the drawing-room, remained to chat a little more and enjoy a glass of Pilsener.

"You may say what you will, Benas, it is more congenial when we are by ourselves," said Mr. Freudenthal.

"You are too exclusive, Isi," said Mrs. Benas. "Surely I am the last who would plead for a mixed choir, since we have been plainly given to understand that our voices do not please; but there is nothing about Dr. Weilen that disturbs our company or seems strange. Even on the first evening he came, he struck the right note, and he seemed one of us. He really is at bottom. One cannot deny one's kin."

"But it took a long time for him to remember," Mr. Friedheim said ironically.

"Only until an opportune moment arrived. How should he have known that the names Lesser and Friedheim belonged to his family? He was still a boy when connections were broken off with his mother's family, and he has never had any occasion to resume the relation," added Mr. Benas. "Friedheim, he knows you through your commentary; Lesser, you, through your 'Order of Bankruptcy,' your names are well known to the lawyer; but that is no reason for him to have supposed you to be his Mishpocheh. It was very evident that he was pleased to discover the additional tie." He laughed jovially. "That's human nature, but the feeling of satisfaction when special honor comes to any member of the family, is particularly developed among us. Even he does not deny this, and why? Estrangement does not change one's inherited nature."

"But habit and education do. Whoever alienates himself and cuts himself off, becomes an exile and a stranger," said Mr. Freudenthal.

"Dr. Weilen is not a case in point. The manner of his coming here is, in fact, an argument against your thesis."

"A mere mood, father, a romantic whim," Hugo said scornfully.

"In such matters your opinion does not count, because your views blind you and make a fanatic of you."

"After all, it is not a matter of great moment that he should have come here," said the Justizrat.

"Years ago you might have said so, but not now. Whoever seeks us now and acknowledges us, belongs to us."

"If you would only free yourself from the habit of considering whatever is connected in the remotest degree with the Jewish question as something of the greatest import. It's really a matter of absolute indifference to me whether a given person comes or goes, how he comes or goes, and what he thinks or does. It's merely a private matter, an individual case."

"Every individual case is at the present time a matter of universal concern," said Hugo, his eyes glowering.

"There we are, before we know it, at the same wearisome discussion. Throw the cat as you will, it always lands on its feet," exclaimed Mr. Benas, angrily.

"The question forces itself upon us, whether we wish it or not," said Mr. Freudenthal, "the clearest proof that it exists; just as a painful sickness reminds the suffering body of its existence. Of what use are morphine injections? Merely a momentary deadening, but the evil is not removed."

"But one gets tired of continually harping on the same old chord," Friedheim answered. "But in the world, by strangers, then in one's own reflections, and finally in the talk of friends, acquaintances, relations, in such social gatherings as this, at Skat, or dinners—everywhere the same dish is served. Occasionally you really long for an injection for the sake of peace."

"Yet there are few to whom the matter has been as vital as to you," said Freudenthal.

"Just because of that. Do you think a wound is healed by constantly tapping it? I use a morphine of my own, my own tried anæsthetic,— strenuous work, untiring activity, and the development of my specialty. This for the world; and for myself,—a quiet family life."

"That has not been your taste always," interrupted Lesser. "You, a politician! A man made for public life! Concerned in every matter of state and city government, always in the public eye."

Earlier in their careers the cousins had harbored slight jealousies in matters of this kind.

"Now we have it again," cried Mr. Friedheim, angrily, rising, "now the sequel will follow: And how did they reward you? Didn't they remind you of the yellow badge your fathers wore? Didn't they wave it before you, a token of past shame, and what is worse, of future shame? How did they thank you for the gift you gave them in your legal work, in your endeavors for the public weal, and so on *ad infinitum?* I know this war cry, and I am not in the mood to-day to hear it again."

Mr. Lesser and Mr. Freudenthal had also arisen.

"Whether you wish to hear it or not, that does not in the least change matters," said Mr. Freudenthal. "And if you should stop up your ears with cotton, you would only deafen yourself temporarily; the trumpet call would sound all the louder."

"I'm entirely satisfied to hear no more of it for a time at least."

"Desire and convenience do not regulate such affairs," said Mr. Lesser, ironically.

"Why not? What's to prevent our getting together comfortably without these endless disputes and excited debates?"

"The fact that the stranger has been in our midst, and we are restless, excited, nervous, like those who live in unrest, without a fixed abiding-place."

All turned toward the speaker; both the women who had followed the conversation in silence, after vain attempts to calm the disputants, and the men, whose tempers were heated by the discussion.

The words seemed to echo from another world,—lamenting, exhorting, warning.

It was Dr. Rosenfeld who had spoken them. The young man sat there deathly pale, as though frightened by his uncalled-for interference in the family quarrel. The whole evening and even during the last conversation he and Hugo had remained quiet, although their faces plainly expressed their interest.

"My dear Henry, you, too, carry matters too far," said Mr. Friedheim, impatiently. "But as our humor is spoilt, and it is late, I think it is best to break up. The fresh December air will cool us off, and we will go home, only to begin over again, at the next opportunity."

"We expect you on Wednesday for Skat," said Mrs. Freudenthal.

"Aha, the session for the next discussion is arranged," Mr. Friedheim laughed.

"Good-by, then, until Wednesday."

"Good-by."

* * *

Hugo and Henry also took their leave to spend an hour at the Café Bauer, where they were to meet several friends.

Mr. and Mrs. Benas and Rita, left alone, went to Mrs. Benas's boudoir.

"It is strange how easily we are carried away when we are among ourselves. Friedheim and Lesser are always ready for a fight. The slightest difference of opinion, and off they go," said Mrs. Benas.

"The curious thing is that at bottom their opinions are not so very different, but argumentation is a racial trait. There's no doubt, we have too much temperament." Mr. Benas smiled, lighting a cigar, and leaning back comfortably in his arm-chair. "I'm curious to know whether Dr. Weilen is such a wrangler as the rest of the Friedländers and the Friedheims," he added, trying to tease his wife.

"I, Joshua? I know others who don't lack the same trait."

"But, Fanny dear, how can you compare us? Generations of practice in the subtle dialectics of the Talmud—that tells. It is not by chance that your family is famous in all intellectual pursuits, while the rest of us, who bear on our escutcheon the rabbit skins and bags of wool carried about by our ancestors, cannot get to be more than mere Geheimer Kommerzienrat."

He liked to refer occasionally to his humble descent from simple merchants; especially when he felt his superiority as a quiet, self-contained man of the world, who could afford to laugh at the irritability and sensitiveness of others. That always put him in a good humor; and Mrs. Benas, well aware of this, fell in with his mood.

"Naturally, Joshua! Geheimer Kommerzienrat, that's nothing! You know you don't believe that. I think we may well be satisfied with one another. Friedländer, Friedheim, and Benas! That's an imposing triple alliance. I think we may be well content."

"And with all that belong to it."

"Even though they quarrel the moment they come together, at the bottom of their hearts they swear by one another and are proud of one another."

"Besides, a bit of argument is entertaining, and brings life into the shindig."

His wife looked at him reproachfully.

"I beg your pardon! I withdraw 'shindig.'"

"Indeed, you ought to be careful, Joe. One's language is bound to deteriorate when one indulges in such vulgar expressions."

"But they're so distinctive and expressive, almost as good as the Jewish intonation."

"Leave them to others."

"Hold on, Fanny. Do you see how I have caught you? Who is exclusive? Who are the others? Who are the others? Pity that Hugo is not here."

He was delighted and amused, and laughed at the embarrassment of his wife. She quickly recovered herself, and answered:

"The others are the vulgar ones, the uncultured, the mob, with whom we have nothing in common, and don't want to have anything in common."

"And the rest say the same of us. Let us have nothing to do with those aliens, those interlopers, those parasites, that ferment, which decomposes the healthy vigorous elements of the Aryan race. That's the gracious, charitable refrain."

"Here we are again at the Jewish question," said Mrs. Benas, somewhat displeased, "we three, here alone."

"Papa, mamma, and the baby," laughed Mr. Benas.

"It's really not funny, Joshua," said Mrs. Benas, earnestly and thoughtfully. "It actually seems as if we could never get rid of it, as if it followed us everywhere. Mr. Friedheim is right. It sits at our table, it accompanies us to social gatherings, to the theatre, and to concert halls; it stands next to us wherever we go in the world, meets us on our travels, and forces itself into our dreams and our prayers."

"You exaggerate, Fannsherl. The imagination and the eloquence of the Friedländers are awakening in you. We know how they think and speak, always in superlatives," he teased good-humoredly, in order to calm her excitement.

"But you see how it is yourself, Joshua. We get here together cozily, in order to chat a bit, to rest ourselves after the strain of entertaining, we have no sinister intentions, in fact, we are ready to reproach our relatives with indiscretion, and before we know it, we are in the thick of it."

"In the soup, *I* should have said," he added, trying to give the talk a jesting turn.

"Joshua, please, don't joke. I am in earnest. Isn't it very sad that all our thoughts should be dominated by this one subject? That we can't free ourselves from it any more? That we can't rise superior to it? That it intimidates us, makes us anxious, petty, serious, and embittered?"

"Yes, dearest, since you ask me to be in earnest, I must agree, that conditions are, indeed, very sad, even though great concessions are still made, have to be made, to us merchants who are in the world of commerce and finance. But for how long? Who knows? A festering wound spreads, despite morphine injections, as Freudenthal says. He could tell tales! One of the most talented of architects, full of spirit and taste, with artistic skill and training seldom met with in his profession, especially here in Berlin, and although he has been a royal Government architect since the year '78, he has been so completely pushed aside that he has been forced to put all his energies into land and suburban speculations out there on the Kurfürstendamm, in the Grunewald suburb, and in the elaborate business-houses on the Leipzigerstrasse. Naturally this brings him a large income, and that is one more reason why his work becomes a reproach."

Mrs. Benas sighed.

"And Friedheim? His capabilities, his thoroughness, and his valuable achievements entitle him to a place in the ministry. Instead of that he has actually reached the exalted point of being Justizrat, a title of seniority like Sanitätsrat among physicians. What difference does it make that as an attorney he has a practice worth one hundred thousand marks? He is ambitious, has aspirations, like all prominent professional men, and finds himself set aside in the prime of his powers. Lesser, too, told me recently that he is going to resign. He has exhausted the last possibility in his career, he cannot hope for further advancement, so he is going to give up official life, devote himself to his scientific researches, and indulge in travel. As soon as Hedwig is married, he and Betty can get away easily. They can leave the boys behind, they have enough money for that."

"That is and will always remain the only thing that gives us independence, and dignity, too," she said bitterly. "We have the money— and then the world is surprised that we strive so persistently to obtain it, hold on to it with such tenacity, and enlarge our fortunes once we have them."

"Nobody wonders at that nowadays. Only the envious and spiteful who have no money themselves. But we may as well admit it; what is true of our own small circle is true everywhere. Well-deserving persons are trammelled in their activities. So far and no farther! Wherever we look, we see them chained to the lowest stages. 'Not beyond the boundary we have mapped out for you,' says the Government. 'You want to climb, you are equipped to be brave mountaineers, you lack nothing you need to reach the summit, neither courage, nor endurance, nor strength. Yet remain below, remain below!' The foot-hills reached at the first spurt, mere child's play for their abilities, are the only heights they are allowed to scale. The way is barred, the natural course of their energies repressed. It is frightful that restrictions other than considerations of capacity should hold back the aspirants; that ostracism should be decreed because of a mere chance adherence to a certain faith."

"Then Hugo and his friends are not so greatly in the wrong as you sometimes declare?" she asked with tense expectancy in her voice.

"No, not in principle, but in their aims. Those are phantoms, fantasies! A dream which foolish boys dream,—and clever women."

Rita had followed her parents' conversation, partly in absent revery, partly with alert interest. "No, you can't get rid of it," she said in a soft, reflective voice. "I myself experienced it this evening, when I was speaking with Dr. Weilen. Suddenly we, too, had arrived at the fateful subject."

"Well, that settles it. You, too—and he!"

Her father kissed her tenderly on her forehead, and added jestingly, "Pray, don't tell Hugo or Henry of this. Good-night, Rita."

"Good-night, papa. Good-night, mamma." She respectfully kissed her parents' hands.

"Sleep well, dear child," her mother said, also kissing her upon her forehead.

*　*　*

On the twenty-third of December a company of young men gathered at the house of Hugo Benas, in his roomy, comfortable study on the second floor. They were in the midst of an exciting debate, when Dr. Henry Rosenfeld entered.

"Why so late, Henry?" one of the young men called to him.

He glanced around at the bright, clear-cut faces. Two decidedly showed the racial type, but in the others the keenest eye could not detect even a slight indication of their origin; they were blonde and blue-eyed, and crowned broad-shouldered figures. Dr. Rosenfeld himself answered this description, and no one would have suspected him to be a Jew.

"We have been expecting you this last half-hour. Magnus told us that you would be here at eight o'clock," said Hugo as he drew out his watch. "It is half-past eight now."

"I was detained by Professor Lisotakis, in the Oriental Seminar." He placed his note-books and volumes on the table and accepted the ready courtesy of one of his companions, who helped him to remove his overcoat.

"Have you been working until now?" Tender solicitude was expressed in Hugo's voice. "Come, sit here," he pointed to a comfortable arm-chair, near the fire-place. "It is very cold this evening, and I am sure you are half-frozen without having noticed it."

They all laughed, but the smile that played about Rosenfeld's lips was a bit forced.

"Perhaps you are right, Hugo. I have been walking fast, lost in thought; and when you think hard, you forget the weather."

"I wager Henry was wandering under cedars and palms on his way here, when in reality he was passing under snow-laden trees along the Linden, through the Tiergarten," laughingly cried out a young man of dark complexion, as he twisted his black moustache, and pushed his gold-rimmed eyeglasses closer to his near-sighted eyes.

He caught a curious glance from Rosenfeld; his deep blue eyes, fixed upon an imaginary point in the far distance, seemed to carry the suggestion of energy and fanaticism.

"That's possible, Sternberg," he answered, "why not?"

"I cannot understand, Sternberg, how you can profane and make a joke of a matter that is sacred to us, the memory of the history of our race," said Hugo.

"Never mind, Hugo, why shouldn't dreams become realities?" said Rosenfeld, with sadness and longing in his voice.

"Not in wanton jests, however."

"A fellow might be allowed a joke now and then," muttered the culprit.

"Hardly! Everything that belongs to our past is too beautiful; and now that it is a departed glory, a lost sanctuary, it is too sad to make mock of. I find it quite out of place to assuage the irritating wounds of the soul with scorn. It is a sign of degeneracy in us to banter and to scoff, and cynically to vulgarize the ridicule and the contempt heaped upon us by others. It is undignified, and makes for disintegration. That's the reason I object to the type of drama in which Jewish manners and peculiarities of the most degenerate and pitiable of our race are exposed on the pillory. They are considered as typical, and people say: 'Look you, such they are!' If I had the authority, I should prohibit them. And then, too, I hate those wretched money jokes, those translations of words from the noble language of our race, which give them a distorted, ambiguous meaning. We are not raised so high out of the mire as to allow ourselves such privileges. We are in the midst of it, in the midst of sorrow and enmity, struggle and defense, and we are far from victory, and we alone are at fault. This lukewarmness, this indifference, this hushing-up, this self-ridicule, they are our misfortune. The tactics of an ostrich! Keep your eyes tight shut! Don't peep! Imagine others are blind! But they are only too well aware of our helplessness, our weakness, our cowardice, our lack of courage. Where could they find a more suitable object on which to let out their bad humor? I tell you, I would do the same thing. He who grovels on the ground, must expect to be spat upon, and he mustn't complain."

His words poured forth in a torrent. He breathed hard, and his face turned ghastly white. Deep silence followed his speech. Sternberg, embarrassed, fingered a book lying before him. His eyeglasses slipped down on his nose, and his near-sighted eyes roved with searching glances from one to the other of the company. At last a young man spoke:

"There's a good deal of truth in what Benas says. We dare not deceive ourselves; indeed, we are the very last to do it, even if one of us does occasionally make a poor joke about it. Every one of us feels the same passionate pain in his soul as Hugo does, and every one is possessed by the same pride and the same enthusiastic desire for a different order of things."

These soothing words made a good impression. Dr. Eric Magnus, a young physician, the scion of a very prominent and wealthy family, always found favor as a peacemaker when differences arose among his comrades. It was he who always did the reconciling, and eased the jars inevitable among young men of such various dispositions. They called him the "Olive Branch," and he was proud of the nickname. "Little Olive Branch is right as usual," said Hugo, and extended his hand to Sternberg across the table.

"I meant no harm, Siegfried; and besides it was quite impersonal, you know that. The subject made me forget myself."

Sternberg was ready to give in; he clasped Hugo's hand heartily. The "Olive Branch" raised his glass, and turning to the two disputants and then to the others, drank to their health:

"*Prosit.*"

"*Prosit,*" they cried as they all touched glasses. And the little unpleasantness that had seemed imminent was averted.

Thereupon Dr. Rosenfeld took a letter from his portfolio, and said: "I have brought a most curious note that I received to-day from Francis Rakenius of Frankfort-on-the-Main. He is visiting his relatives there for a few days, before starting for East Africa. You know that he is a faithful Protestant, the son of a pastor, and belongs to a very pious family. His grandfather was school superintendent, his uncle was the celebrated professor of canonical law at Halle, and the opinion of such a family concerning our status seems to me of some value."

He had spoken in a low voice while unfolding the letter. Then he looked at the assembled company. Interest and expectancy were depicted on the faces of all. They knew that years ago, during the first semesters of their college life, an intimacy had existed between Rosenfeld and Rakenius. They had attended the same lectures, prepared for the same examinations, and received their degree of doctor of philosophy on the same day. Rakenius then went to Halle to continue his special study of theology, and Rosenfeld remained in Berlin. Even as a student Rosenfeld had been much interested in the various schemes to improve the shameful conditions which a continually increasing anti-Semitism had brought about. He attended meetings, joined various societies, at one time was a Zionist, and finally accepted with enthusiasm the idea of providing places of refuge for the persecuted Jews by the foundation of agricultural colonies in Palestine. No one knew whether he harbored greater ideas; but at all events, he changed his views and he gathered about him a considerable following, not only from among the poor, downtrodden sons of the Orient, who, while studying in Berlin, suffered hunger and torment and the scorn and contempt of their Aryan fellow-students, but also from among the young men of the most prominent, wealthy, and respectable families.

There was something winning in Rosenfeld's nature. Everyone who came in contact with him was devoted to him. His very appearance, which suggested endless sweetness despite the strength of his physique, won him immediate sympathy. And his appearance did not belie his disposition,— honest, simple, and modest. But one felt that his amiable manners concealed the energy and the fearlessness of a true demagogue, and, if need be, he would give clear, vigorous, and absolutely truthful expression to his convictions. Of late he had become entirely occupied with questions concerning the Jews. All political and social events he interpreted only in their bearing upon what was dearest to his heart. In this way he had obtained a strong influence over his companions, and he became their leader. Hugo Benas, Eric Magnus, and Siegfried Sternberg were devotedly attached to him; and they formed a circle within their circle, which zealously served the general interest. At meetings they were the spokesmen, peculiarly fitted by education and circumstances, for each one of them, by birth, wealth, and station, could have laid claim to and achieved a good social position, such as is ordinarily open to young physicians, lawyers, and scholars. Yet they had but one aim,—to devote themselves to the cause of their unfortunate, persecuted race. And they spoke of nothing else whenever, as on the present occasion, they met for confidential, friendly intercourse. With some impatience, therefore, they awaited Rosenfeld's communication.

"Let us hear what Rakenius writes," demanded Sternberg. Henry read aloud to them:

"I can perfectly understand your sense of uneasiness, and I sympathize with you. It requires a degree of self-renunciation that cannot be expected, and in my view should never be demanded, of men with proud natures, men of intellect and spirit, men of marked individuality, to suffer what is put upon the Jews. Yet such is the situation, and whether it is justified or not, is a point upon which at this time I do not care to express an opinion. You know how truly devoted I always have been and still am to you. I have never had a better friend, a dearer companion than you. Our friendship was secured by our agreement on the philosophic questions that used to occupy us, by the similarity of our views in regard to things in general, and by our wholly concordant attitude toward the various problems of social life. I need give you no further assurances in regard to that; and whether I separate the personal from the more general view, I am unable to say.

"Ever since you wrote that the Jewish question occupies you to the exclusion of all else, I have been concerning myself with it. In fact it is an insistent issue. It forces itself upon me in my profession, in the world in which I live. You know that I am devoted, body and soul, to my priestly calling, and my attachment grows stronger the more I steep myself in the spirit of the Protestant doctrine. How it is to be deplored that the best among you cannot partake of its blessings; for whoever has had the fortune to call you friend, knows how to value you; and I am just enough to recognize that there must be many other Jews like yourself. But whether it is that you cannot, or that we do not wish it, the result remains the same; and this result cannot be gainsaid. A few days ago, I came across an expression of Feuerbach's, which perhaps gives an explanation of the reproach, often brought against the Jew, of pushing aggressiveness. 'To do away with the meaninglessness of our individual existence,' he says, 'is the purpose of our lives, the motive of our enterprises, the source of our virtues as of our faults and shortcomings. Man has and should have the desire to be individual. He properly desires to attain significance, to achieve a qualitative value. As a mere individual, he is lost like a single drop of water, indistinguishable in the wearisome stream of a meaningless aggregate. If a person loses the interests that express his individuality, if he becomes conscious of the insignificance of his bare personality, he loses the distinction between existence and non-existence, life becomes loathsome, and he ends it in suicide; that is, he annihilates his non-entity. It is natural that this striving for individual distinction comes out most clearly in a class of society socially subordinated, as a foreign race or a religious sect, subject to the persecution of the majority. Everybody wishes to stand for something; and to this end grasps at the best means to secure position or distinction in the domain of science. It is on this account that the Jews form so large a contingent to the student class, and they do not shrink from mediocrity, the consequence of a lack of talent.'

"Ah, my dear Rosenfeld, if each of you could only carry Feuerbach's analysis with you and let it plead for you on your way through life! But even then the world would cry out with Conrad Bolz: 'It is an excuse, but not a good one;' and above all, we do not wish to accept it. For it interferes with us, it restricts us. We do not wish to grant so large a field to others for the development of their individuality, we need the room ourselves. The result would be that the aliens would have to renounce the development of their individuality, their striving for the distinctiveness that raises them above the level of general mediocrity. To this you would not submit; why should you? There is so much talent, so much spirit, so much vigor among your co-religionists. It would be suicide committed by individuals of your race, if they passively submitted to absorption by the mass, instead of saving themselves for the welfare of their own people.

"Whether this end can be attained, I cannot judge. It may be difficult! Exceedingly difficult! But at one time there was One among you who accomplished the most difficult of all things—the salvation of the world.

"If this scheme should prove impracticable, then I can see only one solution: Acknowledge yourselves as disciples of Him who went forth from your midst. Your best, your greatest, your most distinguished men would have to take the lead. Generations may pass before the traces are wiped out, before the recruits are recognized as veterans; but time will bring maturity. If ever you should think otherwise than you do now, then come to me...."

"That is pure proselytizing," Sternberg burst forth.

"You do not know Rakenius," answered Rosenfeld, sadly. "It merely shows how the very best, the most unprejudiced, and the clearest minds among them think."

"And I cannot say that I find the letter remarkably unprejudiced," said Hugo, impatiently.

"But that's the way they think and feel. It crops out even in those that are anxious to understand our peculiarities. Rakenius never gave me the least occasion to mistrust him. He was the one who made the approaches in our friendship, because, as is natural, we are always the ones to hold back for fear of being misunderstood, of being considered aggressive. What he writes is his honest conviction. They know no other solution for our difficulty. But his letter has shown me anew that at least he tries to understand the other man."

"It is always the same story; even our defenders are our accusers," said Magnus, sadly.

"While on the one hand Feuerbach shows our course to be justifiable, he on the other hand admits our inferiority, our mediocrity."

"Among the masses."

"But the masses among the others do not study at all, and so we come back to the same point. Despite mediocrity and weakness we push forward; and that is just what as aliens is not our right."

After further discussion of the topic, Magnus and Sternberg left. Henry and Hugo were alone. Occupied, each with his own thoughts, they remained in silence for some moments. Then Hugo asked his friend with concern in his voice: "Are you tired?"

"O no, just a bit unstrung."

"May I speak to you of another matter this evening?"

"Certainly."

"I am uneasy about Dr. Weilen's intrusion in our family circle. What does he want? What does his interest mean, his familiarity? He comes often, as if he belonged here, like a cousin,—and they like him. All of them—except myself. And I'm afraid—afraid for Rita!"

Henry turned white, he bit his lips, rested his head on his hand, and did not answer.

"What do you think, Henry? You know my sister well. During the lessons in philosophy that you give her, you surely have an opportunity to probe the girl's soul. What do you think?"

"Who dares say he knows another's soul,—especially that of such a sensitive nature as Rita?" he responded hesitatingly. "But do you know, Hugo, I am more tired than I thought I was; I think I'd better go."

"Shall I go with you?"

"No, I thank you. It is late, and there is no reason for your going out into the cold."

"Well, then, until to-morrow."

"Good-night, Hugo."

He went slowly down the stairs. The corridors were still brilliantly lighted. As he reached the hall of the main floor, a servant was holding the door open for Dr. Weilen.

"O, good evening, Dr. Rosenfeld," he greeted him good-humoredly.

"Good evening, Dr. Weilen."

"Hospitality seems to be exercised on all the floors of this house. You have just been with Hugo?"

He nodded in answer, and the two men left the house together.

* * *

It was about eleven o'clock when Dr. Rosenfeld left his friend, and Hugo was surprised when scarcely a quarter of an hour later, some one rapped at his door. Elkish, the old clerk of the firm of Joshua Benas, stepped in. His bachelor dwelling was in a wing of the house. Here his unmarried sister kept house for him according to the strictest Jewish observances. Certain privileges were extended to him as the confidant of the family. The assured devotion of the whimsical old man was the excuse for allowing him to do as he wished. In business he was all conscientiousness, faithfulness, and capability. The younger clerks knew that their weal or their woe lay in his hands, for the Geheimrat took no step in business matters without Elkish's advice. He therefore imagined he had a right to concern himself about family matters as well, and he was good-naturedly allowed his way. The Benases were confident that he held the welfare of their house dearer than his own, and though it was not always possible to yield to his peculiar wishes, his interference was tolerated without great opposition. Jewish homes often harbor such characters, to whom loyalty gives privileges justified by long service, though their manners are not in harmony with the present order of things. Even in the old days in Lissa, Elkish had been a confidant of Benas senior; and this had endeared him to the son, and later to the children of the third generation. To Rita and Hugo he used the language of the most familiar intercourse, and both of them felt a peculiar attachment to him. As children they had spent many an hour daily in his rooms. He and his sister were most ingenious in preparing surprises and pleasures for them, and it was there that they had learnt to know the charm of the old Jewish life. The services of the coming in and the going out of the Sabbath, of the Seder evenings, and of the high festivals, were strictly observed. A lost world was thus brought back to the bright and eager children. In their parents' home the old life was shown sacred respect, but without adherence to ceremonies. In Rita the ceremonies appealed to the imagination, in Hugo to the intellect. To the girl the peculiar customs had been sources of pleasure, but to Hugo of earnest reflection. Rita had frolicked and laughed when Uncle Elkish on such occasions went through the consecrated forms with solemnity and dignity; Hugo, even as a boy, had experienced a feeling of awe for the noble past from which these customs came. So the children had lived in two worlds. Their parents' household was entirely "modern." While Rita and Hugo were quite young children they had discarded—as many others of the Jewish faith had done at the same time—the observances that differentiated them from those of other faiths. When, however, the time came which forced them back upon their own resources, the son and daughter, now grown up, did not find the changed circumstances as strange as they would have, had they not come under Elkish's influence. They appreciated why sacrifices were demanded, and why they should not desert from the ranks of a religion whose principles, founded in a glorious past, formed the bond that held the race together though scattered through all countries. Elkish's importance thus increased in their eyes. Hadn't he been right in holding aloof from the stranger? As a result, he did not feel the repulses under which they suffered so intensely. Hugo was particularly affected, because as a student, soldier, and lawyer, he was brought in constant contact with a Jew-hating world, and exposed to continual mortifications and secret and open attacks. All this embittered him; and he drew closer than ever to the old man, who was inspired alike with great hate for the oppressor and with zeal for the faith. And so Hugo greeted his visitor with sincere pleasure.

"Why so late, Elkish?" he called to him cheerily. "What brings you here? Pity you did not come sooner. You should have heard Dr. Rosenfeld this evening; it would have warmed the cockles of your heart."

"My heart in this old body cries and laments. Hugo, what will it all come to? I'll never laugh again, Hugo, never. With Tzores I shall go to the grave."

"What are you talking about, Elkish? Before that happens, you still have a lot to do; and you really would have been pleased to see our friends here this evening—Dr. Rosenfeld, Dr. Magnus, and Sternberg."

"What do I care about doctors and lawyers when, God forbid, danger threatens us?"

"What danger?"

"Are you blind, Hugoleben, and deaf? Don't you want to see and hear, or don't you really see and hear? On this floor, you form Jewish societies, you and your friends. Rosenfeld talks, and Sternberg scolds, and the 'Olive Branch' hopes, and you think,—but you don't think of what's nearest to you, of what is going on below. Day after day that *Posheh Yisroel*, the aristocratic Herr Regierungsrat, comes and makes himself agreeable, and poses as being one of the Mishpocheh and *Chavrusseh*, and Rita is there, my Ritaleben, and listens to the Chochmes and the brilliant conversation, and gazes at the handsome, noble gentleman .... and .... and...."

"But, Elkish, don't get excited. What's gotten into your head? Papa and mamma are there, and I, too, and very often the other relatives."

"Just because of that! I am not afraid that he will seduce her the way a *Baal-Milchomoh* seduces a *Shicksel*. Such a thing, thank God, does not happen with us Jews. But he will lead her astray with his fine thoughts and noble manners, and his great position, and heaven knows what else, and he will make her forsake her religion, become an apostate as he himself is."

Hugo, himself suspicious of the friendly intercourse growing up between Dr. Weilen and his own family, was alarmed at the old man's outburst.

"You see things too sombrely, Elkish. There have always been people of high position, even Christians, that have visited us."

"Those were original Goyim, dyed in the wool, not such as he, and not related, God forgive me that I must admit it. And when they came, it was for the good dinners, and the fine champagne direct from France. I ought to know, for I paid the bills. Those real Cognacs, and the cigars with fancy bands! A small matter! Herr Geheimrat can well afford it. Why object? We merely shrug our shoulders—and despise them. When they came and made genuflexions, and were never too tired to find us, then they wanted money—much money—for charity, and for monuments, and for foundations, and for all sorts of things—even for churches. Why not? The Jew has always been good enough for that. I never dissuaded your father from such gifts. He still takes my advice occasionally; and when he says, 'I am well advised, Elkish,' then he merely means, 'What is your opinion of the matter, Elkish?' And I have always thought, there is no harm in giving, and surely not in taking. And when those other fellows, the artists, came and told your mother of their paintings and their busts, and invited her to their studios; and made music to the tune of one thousand marks an evening, and some concert tickets besides, I never protested, but I did some thinking, and I wondered what Mr. Mendel Benas of Lissa would have said, had he seen where our good money goes to. But we've grown so great, why should we not give? The time came when they paid us back more than we need. That's all right. Perhaps not for the individual, for he grieved, like your father or like Friedheim or Freudenthal, or all the great folk among the Jews; but it was good for the rest. The Christians began to think that they have a right to be considered, and *we* began to feel we were what we are—Jews."

When Elkish flew into a passion, it was not so easy to calm him. Hugo therefore did not interrupt his harangue, a mixture of indignation, scorn, and disappointment. With most of it he himself agreed, and even though he viewed events from a more modern standpoint, yet at bottom he held the same opinions as the embittered old man. It did not seem strange to Hugo that Elkish had dropped into his native jargon, for the sake of emphasis. He always did so when excited.

"And therefore I always said," he continued, after a short pause, "'Mr. Benas,' I said, 'as you like.' But now I do not say 'as you like.' For this fellow wants not only our money, but our child, too,—our darling Rita."

His voice turned hoarse, and the last words sounded like a plaint.

"Elkish!"

"Yes, yes, Hugo, that's what it is! Why did he never come before? He has been in Berlin a long time, and he's always known who Joshua Benas was, and in what relation he stood to him."

"But a special occasion brought him to us, Uncle Leopold's birthday—"

"Nonsense! That is a pretext! He had to say something. He had it all planned. *He* wishes to celebrate Reb Löbl's birthday! *Oser!* not a word of truth."

"There was no necessity for an excuse to visit us; he knew quite well that my parents would have received him, even if he had only said that he wished to become acquainted with his mother's relatives."

"But the other story sounds better, more romantic. That attracts a young girl like Rita. You may believe me, Hugo. I know her. She has not said a word about him, and she goes about as if in a dream. She used to tell Rosalie and me about everything, about Jedlitzka, with whom she plays, about Skarbina, with whom she paints, about the theatre and the concerts, and the lessons in philosophy with Rosenfeld, and whether 'Olive Branch' dances better than Cohnheim of Bellevue Street. My sister and myself got all our entertainment through her, on Shabbes afternoons, when she came to us, just as when she was a little girl. But she's never spoken a word about him, not a syllable; as if he did not exist. And yet he comes every afternoon to tea, and evenings, and noon; and they meet at the Opera House, by chance, of course, and by chance, too, in the skating rink, on the Rousseau Island. Mlle. Tallieu is always present, and she told my nephew Redlich, who studies French with her. She even told it to him in French."

Hugo listened thoughtfully.

"But, my dear Elkish, there is nothing to be done about it. Papa and mamma have begged me expressly to treat him with the utmost courtesy, even though I found it hard from the very beginning. So I withdraw as far as possible when he comes; because it goes without saying that a man of his station must be met with consideration. There really is something very simple and engaging about him."

"There you have it, there you have it!" wailed Elkish. "It would be much better if you did not withdraw, but remained, and took care that she did not fall in love."

"It wouldn't do any good."

"Why not?"

"Do you believe, Elkish, that a girl like Rita becomes enamored of externals? Because some one pays her compliments, or casts languishing looks at her, which the presence of a third person might hinder?"

"Well, then, with what do girls fall in love?"

"They fall in love with the personality of a man; with his spiritual nature and his appearance, when the two are united in a congenial individuality— in a man who appeals to or supplements their own character, or charms them."

"I do not understand such stuff, Hugo. Thank God, I am not meshugge. But it is enough to make you crazy to think that a good Jewish girl cannot be kept from falling in love with a Posheh Yisroel. I always advised your father to arrange the match with Reinbach of Mannheim. If he had followed my advice, she would have been married long ago; and I am curious, very curious, to know whether in such circumstances it would have occurred to the Regierungsrat to wish to celebrate the birthday of Reb Löb Friedländer."

"But Rita did not care for young Reinbach; and I am sure no one can blame her. Such an arrogant upstart, without any ideals."

"There are some with ideals and some without. Reinbach is so rich that I cannot see why he needs ideals."

"Well, to be sure, Elkish, he cannot buy them. But we need not complain of our financial position, either, and yet we are moved by ideals in our demands and hopes. Or look at Magnus. His father is a millionaire, and yet he thinks of nothing but the fulfilment of our plans. And look at Sternberg, and Rosenfeld, and myself, and others who might pass their lives seeking pleasures of all kinds, instead of worrying over the sorrows of our nation. And here comes a South German dandy, a man about town *à la mode de Paris*, a Jew, the type that is now being persecuted and maligned as never before, and whenever we come to the subject that absorbs us all so much, he curtly remarks, 'Judaism is a misfortune.'"

"That is a phrase, nothing more."

"It seems to me this is not the time for empty phrases," he answered gloomily. "The man that uses them, and uses them with such an air of superiority, is a fool. And that Rita should not accept such a fellow, you should find quite proper."

"I prefer a Jewish fool to a baptized philosopher."

"There are also Jewish philosophers." Henry's fine, pale face suddenly came to his mind. He arose and paced up and down the room lost in thought. Then he said:

"It is very late, Elkish."

"A Jewish philosopher, however, is no good match," he persevered.

"Rita must decide that, not we. So let us go to bed now."

"But, Hugo, you must promise me one thing. Be on your guard,—be on your guard."

He shook the old clerk's hand: "Rest easy, Elkish. I share your fears, and also your dislikes."

"I knew it. That's why I came to you. Good night, Hugo, with God's help all will come out right."

"Let us hope so."

When the door had closed upon the old man, Hugo fetched a deep sigh. It occurred to him how suddenly and apparently for no reason Rosenfeld had left, when the conversation had turned upon Dr. Weilen's intercourse with his family.

"Is it possible that he, too...." He stared fixedly into the burning embers for some time before he put out his lamp, and went to sleep.

* * *

It was the first of January. Rita sat reading in the small, cozy drawing-room. A bright wood fire crackled upon the hearth, lit for cheer only; for the house was well heated otherwise. Rita could not bear a cold and desolate fire-place, especially on a day like this, when the cold out of doors was severe. On such days only a flood of light and warmth could bring comfort indoors. It was hardly four o'clock, but the lamps were lit, and the electric light, shaded by bright bell-shaped glass globes, produced a pleasant effect.

Through the windows draped with costly lace curtains the waning daylight peeped and the flurries of large snow-flakes. Rita put her book aside, and gazed thoughtfully at the falling snow. How beautiful the flakes were!—the white floating crystals, that played at tag, and chased each other, and then fell so silently and so calmly. The snug comfort of a warm room was peculiarly attractive in contrast to the scene outside. Suddenly she thought of those who might be out in the cold. She glanced at the clock; it was almost four o'clock. "Mother must be just arriving now," she said to herself.

"I hope the snowdrifts will not cause delays." She looked worried and arose to go to the window.

At this moment a rap came at the door, and the servant handed her a card, and announced Dr. Weilen.

"Ask him in."

And then he stood before her, and grasped her hand, and pressed it to his lips.

"May I personally repeat the good wishes I sent in writing this morning?"

Early in the day he had sent beautiful flowers with the compliments of the season.

"That is very kind of you," she answered, trying to overcome a slight embarrassment. "I am glad to have the opportunity to return your kind wishes and to thank you. But you must be satisfied with my company to-day. Yesterday my mother decided to take a short journey on which she started this morning, and my father and my brother are not likely to return until dinner time, at six o'clock."

He gazed at her without speaking, and the delicate blush that suffused her face assured him that his unspoken answer was understood.

She knew that he longed to be alone with her, and she also knew that it was for her sake that he came as often as the conventions of polite society allowed. Since he had first appeared among them, several weeks ago, he had called repeatedly, and it was obvious that he felt at home with them. Mr. and Mrs. Benas enjoyed his company. With the ease of the man of the world, and with his confiding manner he had readily made a place for himself. Without overstepping the barriers that his long estrangement from his family had unconsciously raised, he was able to assume a happy mean between the position of a guest and that of a relative. Rita, too, he had been able to win over to his side. She liked to see him, such as he was, partly as one of them, and partly as the formal guest. He had overcome her shyness to such an extent that she accepted him, now as a cousin and again as a visitor. It lent an especial charm to their intercourse, this mingling of intimacy and formality. It attracted him, and even more captivated her. On his arrival it was always the Government official whom she greeted; but when she became interested in the conversation, following his lead, she called him cousin. It was a source of unending delight to him, when, carried away by the excitement of the conversation, she, of her own accord, called him cousin.

"To what happy circumstances do I owe the pleasure of finding you alone on this New Year's Day, so that I may express to you my sincere, heartfelt wishes for your happiness, my dear, dear Rita?"

She sat down at the hearth again, and he placed himself opposite. He looked at her face which, brightened by the reflections from the hearth-fire, and illuminated by her inner excitement, seemed particularly charming.

"Mamma left this morning for Rawitsch, to visit Uncle Leopold; and papa and Hugo are visiting Uncle Friedheim who has been unwell for several days."

He looked at her in astonishment, then he smiled knowingly. "Your mother has gone to Rawitsch, to Uncle Leopold? So unexpectedly? She mentioned nothing of her intention on the day before Christmas, when I was here, although we spoke even more than usual about Uncle Leopold and his birthday."

"Mother decided only yesterday,—there were several things she wished to.... She believed...." She tried in vain to conceal her hesitation.

"In this cold and stormy weather? It must have been quite an important matter."

"O, not at all, Dr. Weilen." Her embarrassment grew. "Mamma has had the intention of going for some time, and the snow came only after her departure. Papa and myself accompanied her to the station, and I am sure that nowadays one travels comfortably and agreeably. The coupé was well-heated, and mamma and her maid had it all to themselves. So few people travel on the holidays. I should have loved to go with her, and by this time she is already at her destination. The train arrives there at 3.28."

At first she spoke with uncertainty, as if searching for an unequivocal purpose for this trip; then her utterance became faster and faster; at the last words she looked at the clock on the mantel. A shepherd and shepherdess of old Dresden china, looking at each other tenderly, held the dial between them.

"Yes, at 3.28," she repeated.

"Rita!" he caught her hand and held it firmly. "Your mother has taken this trip in order to plead for me. She has granted my wish! Quite as a diplomatic ambassador! She wished to intercede for me personally, to be my spokesman, to brush aside scruples and prejudices; to place the strange and unexpected in a proper light; to express her conviction that this desire of mine is not a whim, but a pious longing that has lain dormant in a secret corner of my heart. All this she is going to put forward in my behalf. The confidence that all have in her she will use in my favor. She is going to say to them: 'From frequent intercourse with Victor Weilen, the son of our aunt Goldine, who died at an early age, your youngest sister, Uncle Leopold, the sister of my mother,—from frequent intercourse with him we have the impression that honest feeling leads him to us; that the secret voice of blood-relationship called him, when he discovered that one of the family, the one whose quiet piety, whose honest belief make him appear doubly worthy of honor to those whom life has driven away from their native soil, had attained his ninetieth birthday, and like a patriarch was going to gather his own about him. And on this occasion Victor Weilen, too, wishes to be present.'"

She looked at him in timid bewilderment. She had slowly disengaged her hand from his.

"O yes! But mamma also found it necessary to supervise the arrangements for the celebration personally. There will be so many people to come to the small town. Our relatives there are, of course, helpless; they are not used to such matters. Arrangements will have to be made in advance for the housing and entertainment of the guests.... You see, it is a special festival that is to be celebrated."

"Do you wish to rob me of the delight of my interpretation, Miss Rita?" There was a pained expression in his voice. "All that might have been done by correspondence, but your kind mother in person had to justify and advocate the wish of a stranger to be one of the guests, a stranger, yet one of their own blood. For this the winter's journey, to-day, on New Year's Day, which people like to celebrate together at home. Am I right, Rita?"

"Yes," she answered simply.

It seemed impossible to her to plead further excuses after he had discovered the honest truth.

Neither spoke for some time. He gazed at her bowed head. The silence was eloquent of inner sympathy between them. The intense quiet of the room was disturbed only by the crackling of the wood fire. It cast red, quivering reflections across the light carpet covering the floor, and glanced brightly adown the girl's dress.

After a few moments during which they were sunk in thought, he said: "I know your mother will succeed in realizing my wish. She is a good spokesman. And I will be near you on that day, Rita—near you!"

And as though unable any longer to control his tumultuous feelings he jumped up, took her in his arms, and whispered softly in her ears, "My Rita!"

She rested upon his bosom, as if stunned, quivering with blissful joy. The uncertainty and misgiving that had troubled her heart throughout these many weeks was now converted into a happy reality. He loved her! He! He raised her bowed head and read the confession of her love in the eyes that looked at him in pure radiance. Deep emotion took possession of him. She loved him with the love that springs up in the sweet, secret longings, in the pure maidenly fervor, in the rare, modest timidity of the daughters of that people from which he had at one time turned away.

As if his thoughts had been transferred to her, she slowly disengaged herself from his arms, hid her face in her hands, and relieved the oppression of her soul in tears. He led her back to the place from which he had so impetuously drawn her, seated her, then kneeled before her, and embraced her softly, tenderly. "Rita, dear sweet Rita, my precious child. Why do you cry? What makes you sad? What frightens you?"

"Happiness."

He drew her to him again passionately, and said: "You shall learn to know this happiness in all its joy. It will exalt you, not sadden you."

"You forget what separates us," she stammered, suddenly alarmed, and tried to free herself from his arms.

He started violently. Then he threw his head back with a proud, victorious gesture, and, caressing her, he said in a firm voice: "That which separated us, draws us together, my love, my sweet love!" She clung to his neck, and without resistance she gave herself up to his kisses.

* * *

At dinner, Rita, to conceal from her father and Hugo the cause of her quiet and reserve, pleaded a headache. She merely mentioned the visit of Dr. Weilen; he had come to pay his New Year's call. Hugo looked at her so searchingly that she blushed, and turned away from his gaze.

"Did you explain to him that we no longer keep open house, since we have plainly been given to understand that we, citizens of a lower estate, have no right to and no part in the holidays of the others?" Deep resentment lay in his words.

She looked at him as though her thoughts were of another world, while her father said in irritation: "Can't you grant us a moment's respite from your indignation and your scorn? You display your malice at every opportunity. It is really ridiculous for you to ask Rita whether she met the politeness of a visitor with such an unpleasant reception."

Rita cast a grateful glance at her father; her eyes shone with the brightness of suppressed tears.

"It is enough that we conduct ourselves as our injured pride demands, but always to throw it up to others is improper and stupid. I tell you those were pleasanter and happier times when we used to celebrate the New Year's eve with a ball, and then the next morning received congratulations, and in the evening, instead of sitting sadly alone as we three are, there was a gathering of gay friends for a dinner."

"They may have been gayer times," said Hugo, nettled, "more amusing, too, and more comfortable, but they were only transient. They were in a condescending mood, and because of an amiable caprice on their part we were allowed to celebrate their feast days with them, and to take part, humbly, in certain civic and public holidays. But religion, despite all, raised an impassable wall between us and them. We were allowed to enjoy pageants, illuminations, parades, patriotic celebrations of all kinds, and then Christmas and New Year, when you're called upon to give in charity. How tolerant! O, how liberal! O, how I hate that word. Sufferance I call it. Sufferance! To be tolerated! You're kindly tolerated, partly as a participant, partly as an observer. And you're perfectly aware that you may be pushed aside at any moment when found *de trop* or too forward. It surely is a thousand times better to be as we are now; without the loud gayety of people to whom at bottom we are strange, and must always remain so. I remember, during my upper class days, the last formal New Year's dinner at this house, how Herr von Knesebeck proposed a toast to the Emperor coupled with the toast for the New Year. And how jovially and with what amiable condescension the attorney-general, Herr von Uckermarck, proposed a toast to mother. What an honor! And the way in which you welcomed the guests, the honored friends of the house—strangers then, to-day, and forever! What led them to us was not our company, but the choice pleasures and the agreeable times our money afforded. And to-day they dispense with all that. It would be impossible to get the best of them to come to us now; but the best of us are those who gratefully reject the honor."

His father was visibly annoyed, and Rita looked anxiously at her brother, who seemed particularly harsh and relentless. If he suspected! A dread possessed her, and pallor overspread her face. The dinner passed off in no very pleasant mood. The three missed the conciliating gentleness of the mother, who shared the son's views without his rancor, and who had opened her husband's eyes to the altered social conditions, while yet appreciating and sympathizing with his regret over the sad changes.

Everyone was glad to have the meal over. Rita excused herself at once. Hugo and his father could find no congenial topic for conversation; and so the first day of the new year drew to an unhappy end.

* * *

The next morning Rita received a letter. She was at breakfast with Mlle. Tallieu and could with difficulty conceal the excitement into which the reception of the letter had thrown her. Fortunately her companion was absorbed in the "Figaro," and paid no attention to Rita, who was thus able to hide the letter in her pocket without its being noticed.

"*De maman?*" she asked, without looking up from her journal.

"*Ceça!*" Rita answered in a low voice.

"*Oh! ce pauvre Henry .... pauvre! Il est mort .... mon dieu! Quel malheur pour ma grande patrie .... cette canaille de D .... C'est vraiment .... cette blamage irréparable.*"

Rita arose. She was accustomed to hear Mlle. Tallieu grow enthusiastic, one day over Zola's "*J'accuse,*" and the next day equally so for *l'armée.* One of the uncultured or rather half-cultured, she was swayed by the force of pathos, and was ever of the opinion of others, if they were forcibly expressed.

At all events Mademoiselle was at this moment fully occupied and well provided. There was an abundance of sliced meat on the table, plenty of marmalade, and other good things; the tea-pot was bubbling; and Rita could hope to remain undisturbed for a long time. She stepped into her mother's room, and, with a timid glance at the "family tree," she sat down to read her letter. Her heart was beating violently, and the sheets rustled in her trembling hands. Several minutes passed before she could gain sufficient self-possession to look at the writing. The words swam before her sight:

"My dear, precious girl, my Rita, my bride! This word fills me with delight, and I know it awakens an echo in your heart; you say it softly to yourself, and you are filled with bride-like thoughts, thoughts that belong to me. Whatever might interfere with the union of our hearts from without, within us reigns love, joy, hope. I know I want to win and possess you, and I know you are willing to belong to me.

"Need I beg your pardon for giving in to the impulsive joy of my heart, to the violent longing of my soul, for not waiting to sue for you soberly and sensibly, as is proper for a man so much older than you are, but stormed you with a youth's love of conquest, throwing prudence to the winds, and scorning careful consideration? I was young again when I saw you before me yesterday in the sweet loveliness of your youth, and I shall be young so long as your love remains the fountain of youth in my soul.

"Do you want to know how it came about? I might answer you, 'Do not ask, be sensible only of the strong, exulting love that arose within us as a marvellous, convincing, dominant fact, as a law of nature.' But I see your earnest, wise eyes, which in the past weeks have rested searchingly upon me so often,—I see them before me in all their sincerity, their sweetness, their purity; and it seems to me that I must explain to the little interrogator all about myself and how it happened.

"You know, my love, how I was left alone in the world at an early age. Without father or mother, having no connections or relatives—quite orphaned; but healthy, full of vigor, happy and independent in every way. And all at an age in which one is in need of love, in need of wise guidance, of intimate intercourse with congenial spirits and the home feeling of a large family, the feeling inborn in the sons and daughters of our race, because it is their only home. But I was quite homeless! With the fearless courage of youth I decided to found a home for myself. It was not difficult for me; my independence, my large income, and perhaps, too, my personal abilities, admitted me to the best society. At the University, among my fellow-students, in the homes of my teachers, I was considered, and I felt myself to be as one of them. Nothing stood between us, nothing tangible, nothing out-spoken. Neither my external appearance, nor my interests distinguished me from them,—so entirely had I become a part of their world. There never came a word from the other world within to recall me to my true self. I knew nothing of my former life; no recollection flitted through my mind, because nothing happened to awaken me; and the soft voices that may have made themselves heard occasionally in the early years, were entirely quieted as the new life attracted me and seemed to wipe out the past. I had entirely forgotten at that time to what faith I belonged, and my friends surely never thought of it. One of them especially attracted me. He was two years older than myself—a talented and refined man. Like myself he was alone in the world and independent. That was the circumstance that led us to a sincere friendship. He was a devout Catholic, and after my examinations we journeyed together to Rome. There, under the overpowering impressions of his art-inspiring belief, we were drawn still closer together. Finally the wish was born in me to share with him the faith that was the basis of his inner life, and which he, I know not whether consciously or unconsciously, had nurtured in me, and had brought to fruitage.

"Think of it, my wise, good girl, how young I was then, how enthusiastic, how entirely I had dedicated myself to friendship, and how easy it was for me to succumb to the magic and mystery of a cult whose splendors and associations, there in Rome itself, possessed us heart and soul. Think of it and you will understand me. The reasons that brought me to the momentous decision were not of a practical kind. I took the step in a state of ecstatic excitement and romantic enthusiasm. I had nothing to forsake, for I possessed nothing that had to be sacrificed for the new faith—neither father, nor mother, nor family,—nothing except my own self, and that belonged to the forces that were then mightiest in me: friendship and imagination. The recollection of an incident of those days comes to me with such remarkable clearness that I will tell you of it. It was the only thing that reminded me of my youth, passed under such wholly unlike circumstances. A few days after the fateful step we were in the galleries of the Vatican. I had again become entranced by the glories of Raphael. Suddenly my eye was caught by a portrait in an adjoining corridor. It was the tall, lean figure of a man who was resting his head in his hand, and looked up thoughtfully from an open book lying before him. In the deeply furrowed countenance a meditative, mild seriousness. Eyes expressing endless goodness. A questioning look in them, questioning about the thousand riddles of the universe. The hand resting upon the book was especially remarkable. It spoke a language of its own. Its lines and shape expressed tenderness, gentleness, kindness, as if it could dispense only blessings.

"I was spell-bound, and could not tear myself away from the picture. There was something familiar in it, as if it were a greeting, a reminder from my youth. Suddenly the thing was clear to me. This man, whose characteristic features unmistakably showed him to be an old Jew looking up from his Talmud, and pondering its enigmatic wisdom, reminded me of my uncle Leopold Friedländer. In a flash the whole scene came before me: how he pored over his Talmud when, led by my mother, I came before him with childlike awe; and how he looked up from his volume and regarded me so kindly, so meditatively, exactly like the man before me in the picture. And while I reeled off what I knew of Hebrew lore, he leaned his head upon his left hand, and his right was placed on his book; then he raised his hand and laid it in blessing upon my head, and the tender lips spoke the Hebrew words of the benediction. It seemed to me as if I heard again the soft, insistent voice; and as if the high-vaulted corridors of the Vatican were transformed into the low, simple room of the Jew's house at Rawitsch. I was as one in a dream. It made a strong impression upon me. Like one possessed I gazed at the picture, and I believe my lips mumbled half-aloud 'Yevorechecho Adonay ve-yishmerecho.' Never since that day have the words left my memory. They remain like a faint echo in my soul. Suddenly I felt a hand upon my shoulder. 'A fine picture, is it not,' said Francis to me, 'this Hebrew of the sixteenth century? I believe he was a Portuguese Jew, who was exiled to some Italian Ghetto, to Trastevere or the Ghetto Vecchio of Venice. Somewhere or other the artist came upon this fine, characteristic head, whose portrait places him amongst the immortals, although his very name is uncertain. He belongs to the Florentine school, possibly a pupil of Del Sarto. The realistic expression of the hand suggests Master Andrea himself; or it may have been Pontormo, or Puligo; at all events, a masterly painter.' While my friend gave these explanations, I had time to recover myself, but it was with difficulty that I threw off the spell of my imagination. So it was a Portuguese Rabbi of the sixteenth century, not my uncle Leopold! And yet he.... I knew it positively. Perhaps there was a talisman bequeathed from one to the other that made these Talmudic scholars of all times so much alike; or was it the Law, to which they devoted themselves with like zeal? Or the similarity of their attitude toward life? Or the tradition that remained unaltered through the centuries? When we left the Vatican soon after I could not dismiss the thought that my uncle Leopold Friedländer had a place among the portraits of the Vatican Gallery.

"Years passed. The incidents of those days had long been forgotten. I was drawn into the great and mighty currents of life. I enjoyed it to the full. After the completion of my examinations for the assessorship, my friends at Bonn advised me to enter the service of the Government. There was nothing to prevent me, and the position offered me was quite to my liking, and satisfied the ambitions then mastering me. With the death of Francis Siebert a great void had come into my life; he had died of typhoid fever on a journey of investigation. In the stormy come and go of life, in the restless haste of existence, such things happen daily; and although painfully shocked by his death, I continued my way. It came at a time in my life when I was battling with a great inner struggle that made me wholly self-centered. I prefer not to speak of this to you, at least not to-day. But one thing I may tell you, the experience did not make me unworthy of you. Conflict and suffering do not degrade a man, and whatever fails to overcome us, makes us all the stronger. But I became more and more lonely, and I fell into the habit of thinking that it was my lot in life to be lonely. I tried to be content alone. It seemed the easier for me since my career was a happy one and gave me contentment; and so did the kind of life it brought with it. I resigned myself to remaining a bachelor. So much of the married life of my friends as had come under my observation did not make me regret that I had renounced it. My calling, my books, my journeys, gave me sufficient satisfaction. I avoided social gatherings as far as my position allowed me to. In this way, time passed in work and recreation, and the even tenor of my days brought me comfort and satisfaction. There were many hours in which this exclusiveness seemed very pleasant to me; and the longing for intimate fellowship with others grew ever weaker.

"Then, a few weeks ago, I happened upon the notice of Rabbi Friedländer's ninetieth birthday. The rest you know. What you do not know, is that on my desk, where I had found the journal containing the notice, I seemed suddenly to see the portrait of the Vatican before me; and an unaccountable association of ideas made me see myself standing before it, not as I was in Rome, but as a small boy before the old man, whom I thought I had found anew in the portrait—in the presence of the devout, kindly man, as he sat poring over his book in his humble room. And then I heard the words of the blessing again—I felt them in my heart, the heart of an experienced, mature man,—and all in the language of my childhood, the language of the childhood of my race. And suddenly the world vanished from before me, the modern world that claimed me, and the old arose in the clear light of holy recollections. Father, mother, the whole family came back to life within me! Then I sought your family, sought you! And how I found all of you—how I found you—

"The subtle charm of true family happiness, the aristocratic security of a settled life, entranced me, mingled though they were with secret anguish over the unjust, the foolish prejudices under which the Jewish community suffers. Such depth of feeling underlies the splendor of your life. There is something so cheerful, so intimate among you. On the very first evening I felt at home with you. Your wise, able father, your noble, sensitive mother, your brother with his splendid vindictiveness, and his proud ideals, all interested me as something new, strange, and yet familiar.

"I had never known a Jewish home of refinement and respectability; I did not realize how such home-life had developed in spite of the unfriendliness and the slights that beset it, and in the midst of hostility that seeks its very destruction. Your friends are of the same admirable type. The men serious, capable, intellectually distinguished, and prominent in their various callings; the women bright, artistically gifted, beautiful; the young people ambitious, well-educated, impressionable, enthusiastic. So I learned to know you and your kin,—my kin. May many be like you, I say to myself. Among the Jews are all too many who under oppression and necessity cannot develop. But how could it be otherwise? By the side of the few, one always finds the masses; by the side of the elect, the average.

"And now you, my girl, my precious Rita, you have seen how your sweet disposition has influenced me, how it awakened within me new and happy feelings, how my very soul goes out in longing to you. I have regained my youth, and it calls to me exultantly: 'Return to your own!'

"These are my confessions. It does me a world of good to be allowed to speak to you in this way; and now you will comprehend why it was that I could not restrain myself, but had to take you in my arms, in the happy assurance that you were willing to be mine.

"Have courage! I will never give you up, and we shall surmount all the difficulties they may put in our way. I shall see you again when your mother returns, and I may be allowed to come. Have faith in me!

Victor."

Tears streamed down Rita's face. He had laid bare his soul to her. She remained for a long time lost in thought, considering what had best be done. She did not conceal from herself that her marriage with Dr. Weilen would encounter strong opposition; that disquiet, excitement, and heartache would enter into her peaceful home when the relation between her and Victor was known. Her father's opposition would be the easiest to overcome, but her mother's? And Hugo's? And Elkish's? And the rest of the relatives? And herself? Was there no inward protest against what she was about to do? Now in these saddest of times, to tear herself away from those who suffered and struggled?

An inexpressible fear possessed her. If only her mother were back at home! Disquieting thoughts again besieged her. How happy she might have been, to love a man like Dr. Weilen, to be loved by him! And now alarm in her hopes, doubt in her wishes. She arose slowly and went to her room, and locked the letter in her desk.

* * *

On the fourth of January Mrs. Benas returned. She was in good spirits, and she had found her uncle hale and hearty. Her relatives in the little town were already excited over the coming event, and busy planning and preparing for it. This year *Pesach* came early. The birthday, according to Jewish reckoning, was on the twenty-sixth day of March, the first day of the festival. She told them that in Rawitsch all arrangements had been made for a celebration on a grand scale. Whatever could not be obtained at Rawitsch was to be ordered from Berlin. Arrangements were all the more complicated because of the Passover observances; but not one of the peculiar customs was to be slighted; everything was to go on as usual on this holiday. The great number of the family who would be present necessitated especial provision for the Seder evening celebration and the days succeeding. It was a mere question of expense, and that need not be considered. On the contrary, it was a pleasant feature, that the unusual event would take place amid unusual circumstances, and instead of bread and cake and the every-day dishes, unleavened bread would be eaten. The distinctive festival, as it has survived in unchanged form, but added glamour to the ninetieth birthday celebration of Uncle Leopold.

The family were gathered at their evening meal when Mrs. Benas reported on her trip. With happy eagerness she told of her visit, how she found everyone, and what were their plans.

"But, Fanny, dearest," teased her husband, "do you realize that you are to feed sixty people on *Matzoth*, and for two entire days! Because, you know, no one may leave before the evening of the second day of the holiday."

"Everything has been taken into consideration," she answered good-humoredly. "Do not worry, Joshua, you won't go hungry, and neither will the others. All kinds of nice things, even the finest pastry can be made out of Matzoth and Matzoth meal—cakes and tarts, and dipped Matzoth and *Chrimsel*, the specialties of the season, and the rest of the delicacies. You're no scorner of the good things of life, and you will enjoy eating these dishes again."

"I'll enjoy the indigestion, too, I warrant. But you're right, dearest, those fine dishes are as unforgettable as they are indigestible, and I am quite ready to risk a Karlsbad Kur in May, in order to eat properly in March."

"It will not be so bad as all that. We shall be careful to combine the prescribed with the palatable. And oh! children, it will be beautiful; I am happy about it now. It will be an occasion on which I shall gladly show what and who we are—we Friedländers."

"Now, don't forget the rest of us," her husband bantered.

"The rest of you belong to us, too," she answered with emphasis. "That's just what constitutes the greatness and the strength of the Jewish family— that it grasps so firmly whatever is attached to it. You cannot imagine who all are coming to this celebration in Rawitsch. Some relatives have announced their coming whose names you hardly know, in addition to those in direct descent from Rabbi Akiba. They are descendants of the brothers and sisters of Rabbi Akiba. Then there will be the relations, grandchildren and great-grandchildren of the sisters and brothers of our grandfather. From the letters received in Rawitsch they would not have been able to trace these relationships, if Uncle Leopold's wonderful memory had not helped to place them. It would have been best if we had had our 'family tree' there as a help in recalling them."

Her husband was much amused at Mrs. Benas's pride and zeal. He had not seen her in so happy a frame of mind since a long time. When she was telling of her trip, he felt himself transplanted back to his youth. He saw before his mind's eye the Seder in the house of his own parents, with the consecration and devout importance at that time attached to the various customs. And a deep emotion stirred this man, usually so cool and skeptical.

"But, tell me, I should really like to know how they will manage. It is no small matter; for instance, at the Seder, how many do you expect?"

"Well, pay attention, Joe, and you children, too," she turned to Rita and Hugo, who had followed her report with interest. "I'll tell you the whole programme. We expect from fifty to sixty persons. Of these the ten or fifteen who are extremely orthodox will lodge with the relatives of Uncle Leopold's wife. They are the sons and a daughter of his deceased nephew. These three families are wealthy and keep a strictly orthodox household, as do most in the town. So the pious ones can be comfortably housed there, and need have no fears on the score of religious observances. The rest will be lodged in the comfortable inn on the market place. I looked at the rooms there, and they are quite possible, allowing for the sort of place Rawitsch is."

"Well, no one will expect to be provided with the accommodations of the 'Kaiserhof' or the 'Palace Hotel.'"

"Certainly not," she laughed, "but there will be compensations. And now, don't interrupt again, Joshua, else I will lose—"

"The thread of the strategical plans for the invasion of Rawitsch!"

"Joshua!" She assumed an injured air.

"But, my dear girl, don't you see how delighted I myself am with all this? The most serious things can stand a bit of joking; but now I'll be real quiet, as well-behaved as Hugo and Rita, and all good children when they are having things explained to them. Well, *avanti.*"

She hesitated an imperceptible moment, and then continued: "Some of the most prominent families, among others the president of the congregation, offered to entertain some of the guests. In an unusual case like this we may avail ourselves of such invitations. They are the friends and acquaintances of the Friedländer family; and besides the whole congregation considers—"

"*Khille* is the proper term in this case," he laughingly suggested.

"Well, then, the whole Khille, yes, the whole town, considers this day of honor to Uncle Leopold as its own."

She knew that much depth of feeling lay hidden in her husband's jests.

"These outsiders, too, are planning to confer especial honors upon him. At all events, the freedom of the city will be extended to him, for his philanthropy embraces all without distinction of religious belief."

"Then perhaps it might be appropriate for us to found 'The Leopold Friedländer Home for Widows and Orphans' on that day, too?"

She looked at him gratefully, and reached her hand across the table to him. He had not spoken to her of this plan. Obeying a generous impulse suggested by her words, he proposed it as something self-evident.

"With a capital of about one hundred thousand marks?"

"Joshua!" her voice trembled with deep excitement. Hugo and Rita regarded their father in astonishment.

"O papa," the girl said softly in gratitude; while Hugo showed the pride he felt in his father, who had decided upon the large sum without hesitation, and then, as if it were a mere aside, Mr. Benas continued: "The main thing is to assemble as large a number as possible in Rawitsch, and to be sure that in respect to lodging everything is well arranged. Now will follow the report of the commissariat: Mrs. Benas has the floor."

His good humor infected his wife.

"Well, in regard to food. I shall send a capable Jewish cook, who knows all about keeping *kosher*. There will be people to help her in Rawitsch. A new table service will have to be bought,—that I attend to, here, and also whatever is necessary to complete the silver service."

"You will provide, then, as I judge, a complete Passover service for sixty persons. And what is to become of all of it afterwards?"

"I have not thought of that yet. But it will not be wasted."

"Suppose each one were to receive his own service to take home as a souvenir?"

She and the children laughed gayly.

"That would not be so bad."

"And for us quite worth the while, we should return with four new sets of table service."

With an expression of content, he glanced at the costly silver service on the tea-table at which they were seated.

"That's what I have been wishing for a long time; and if we are fortunate, we may receive a soup tureen with it."

"You're a tease, Joshua. Why should there not be souvenirs of the day?"

"But not exactly silver forks and knives. It might lead to sad complications." Then as if an idea had suddenly occurred to him, he continued, "Do you know, Fanny, leave it all to me. What would you think if I bought so beautiful and valuable a silver service that it might be used after the festival for Rita's future household? It would be fine to own silver dedicated on such an occasion. What do you think of it, Rita?"

At her father's words Rita turned pale. "O papa!" she stammered. She felt Hugo's eyes staring at her, and the blood rushed back to her cheeks.

"You need not get white and red at the idea. The silver service might suggest a groom, but no one forces you to accept him." He was amused at his daughter's confusion. "At all events, you are of an age to justify such thoughts. However, I am quite ready to save this silver treasure for you in my safe just as long as you want.

"Joe, if you don't stop joking, we shall never finish. First I am the butt, then Rita. But Rita," she turned to her, "you know your father, and know he is never happier than when he's teasing us. You need not feel embarrassed by what he says. But you really do look as if you had never heard of a young girl of twenty marrying." While her mother was talking, Rita tried to regain her self-possession.

"Mamma, it was only so curious,—the ideas that papa has—this silver."

"Five dozen; everything necessary for sixty persons. Quite complete. Renaissance, rococo, or Empire ... perhaps the English style pleases you better?" he asked in fun.

"Please, Joshua, do let the poor child alone. I should really like to consider the matter seriously."

"Well, then, to be quite serious; the question of the arrangements for the table is settled, and with that everything, I believe. You attend to the dishes; they need not exactly be Limoges or old Vienna. The silver I shall see about, with an idea to future use. I have no doubt, good things will go into the dishes, and enough, too. At such family festivals there is always enough and to spare. The fish and fowl of the region are famous, and other things, too. The Matzoth will be baked especially for us, and Gregorovius, of Unter den Linden, shall provide the apples for the *Charoseth*. Everything will be excellently arranged, I mean it seriously. And I am looking forward to the festival with much pleasure. Whatever is intrusted to Fanny Benas, *née* Friedheim, of the family of Akiba Friedländer, can only be good and blessed."

The last words were spoken gravely, with deep feeling. He arose, took his wife's hand and kissed it.

"But you have not told us about one thing—about the chief reason for your going. What do the relatives think of Dr. Weilen's wish?"

The children awaited their mother's answer in breathless expectation. Hugo's eyes were fastened with sullen looks on his mother's lips; Rita looked shy and anxious. It seemed to her as though her heart had stopped beating, and a choking sensation caught her at the throat.

"I am decidedly curious to know what was your success."

"He may come!"

The face and attitude of the Geheimrat showed decided interest.

"Really? How interesting! I was very doubtful of the issue."

But Hugo clenched his fist, and said vehemently: "Impossible! How could they consent? He will spoil the holiness of the days. What does he want there? What does he wish of us? A stranger!"

Rita started at her brother's words. His harsh, unfriendly attitude hurt her; but she maintained her self-possession through the very resentment they aroused; she suppressed the sigh that betokened her inner struggle, and catching her breath, she said: "He is no stranger!"

"That seems to have been the opinion of the rest of the family," Mr. Benas said to his son, "and it is really time, Hugo, that you put an end to your childish and uncalled-for prejudice against Dr. Weilen. His personality certainly gives no occasion for such feeling, and he does not encroach upon your wishes and theories. He seems to me the last man to stand in your way."

Rita gave her father a look of gratitude.

"He has no right to, and never shall have," Hugo answered angrily.

"You spoil everything with your intolerance. And now enough. I'd much rather hear what the pious old man thinks in his mild wisdom than listen to the opinions of a hard, callow youth in his folly."

Hugo ground his teeth, and refrained from answering.

"Well, Fanny, how did it go?"

"At first it seemed very strange to the various members of the family. The oldest son of Uncle Leopold, with whom he is living, Cousin Isidor, and his wife Hannah, could not at first comprehend what the question was about. Cousin Isidor is already past seventy, and the horizon of his wife does not extend beyond the line connecting her room and the synagogue."

Involuntarily she glanced at Hugo before she continued: "Considering the narrow existence they lead, it is not to be wondered at. The daughters of Uncle Leopold, Friederike and Rebecca, and their husbands were also not a little astonished. I found their children, a few of whom have remained at home, equally unsympathetic; but all of them yielded without objection to the authority of Uncle Leopold, who lives among them like a patriarch. He said: 'If Fanny Benas, the daughter of my brother-in-law Friedheim of Rogasen, and of my sister Henrietta, pleads for him, then he is surely a good man. And my sister Goldine, his mother, was the darling of my mother and my father, Zichrono livrochoh. She was named after her grandmother, Golde Freidchen, the wife of our grandfather, the Gaon Rabbi Akiba, Zecher Zaddik livrochoh. Goldine was the youngest of us fourteen children, and the first to die; and if her son wishes to come to me, the oldest and only one, who, boruch ha-Shem, is still here, and if I have the fortune to survive until the day of the celebration, then he shall come. He shall come with the rest of you, and he shall rejoice with you. And I shall see the only child of my beloved sister Goldine.' Aunt Riekel softly interrupted: 'But he is baptized!' An indescribable look of pain moved his withered old face; but it lasted only for a few moments, and then he answered in a mild voice: 'If he wishes to come, he shall come. Perhaps Golde Freidchen has interceded for her great-grandchild that he should find his way back to the fold. For if a Jew is baptized, and he calls out in his hour of death, Shema Yisroel, he shall be accounted a Jew! Shall I be more severe than Shem Yisborach?' Profound humility and goodness were expressed in his words; and no one contradicted him."

Mrs. Benas's recital was received in silence. She continued: "The person expected is evidently not the Regierungsrat Dr. Weilen, but the son of Aunt Goldine, the youngest sister of Uncle Leopold Friedländer."

"And as such he'll come to them," said Rita, dreamily. She had listened to her mother's tale as to a revelation. It seemed to her thirsting soul like a miracle from far distant times, and the words forced themselves to her lips involuntarily.

"Do you believe that, also?" asked Mr. Benas of his wife.

"I am convinced a man such as he is will strike the right note."

"So that is settled, too; and we may look forward to the celebration without concern. You must let Dr. Weilen know the result of your intercession."

"I shall write to him to-morrow."

* * *

On the following afternoon Mrs. Benas was sitting in her room, looking meditatively before her, an expression of melancholy in her sweet, refined face. Rita had just left her. Mother and daughter had experienced an hour of profound agitation; Rita had sought her in order to confess her love for Victor. Trembling and hesitating, she confided in her mother as in a friend; how the feeling had been awakened on the very first evening, when he referred to his loneliness, and how it had gradually grown, the more she saw of him. His amiable, open-hearted disposition had appealed to her; but above all his confiding intimacy which had found so little encouragement. Hugo, in fact, had often spurned him rudely. It had always pained her to see a man, by nature so proud and gentlemanly, accept these rebuffs with patience and forbearance. Once, when she tried to excuse Hugo, he had said: "I understand his grief and indignation, and so I can forgive him. He must have suffered much before he arrived at a state of such intense resentment as to make him see an enemy in everyone with different opinions from his own. But some day we may find a point of contact; and until then his young anger shall not drive me away from the home of your parents, a home that has grown dear to me,—and from you, Rita." Since that time a secret understanding had existed between them. They had said nothing to each other; but she knew that he grew dearer to her from day to day. She was happy when he came, and missed him when he stayed away. She knew that he loved her; she knew it through the delicate and subtle sensitiveness that exalts the soul of a young girl in this phase of her life, endows her with intuitions, and makes each slightest impulse rich with meaning. Then came that sacred hour of the New Year's Day,—and his letter. She confessed all to her mother, gradually overcoming the timidity and fear with which she had begun her recital, until her confession grew into a veritable pæan of love. Her mother was deeply moved. At the moment she had no thought of the obstacles in the way of such a connection; she thought only of the happiness of her child. Then she read Dr. Weilen's letter. Rita's eyes rested on her mother's face to note the effect of his confessions. Mrs. Benas was profoundly touched. At first it merely interested her greatly, then it stirred her emotions. When she finished tears stood in her eyes. Rita, sobbing in mingled joy and sorrow, sought refuge in her mother's arms.

What would be the outcome of it all? For the present Mrs. Benas could give no answer. But she quieted her, lovingly caressed the cheeks wet with streaming tears, and urged her to be calm. Nothing must be done precipitately, particularly because of the coming celebration. Such consideration was due to the old sage to whom this day was to be dedicated. Whatsoever might disturb the harmony, or cause bad humor or disquietude must be avoided. Surely she was not asking too much in expressing the wish that until after the celebration no decision should be reached. In the meantime, things must remain as they were; and she was convinced, a man like Dr. Weilen, wise and prudent, would acquiesce.

"But he may visit us?" Rita anxiously questioned.

"Certainly; he may come as before."

"And shall I say nothing to him, mamma? Not speak to him of his letter? Not of all I think and feel?"

"I can't prescribe as to that, dear child. But I trust your tact. The private understanding that has existed between you two until now, I do not want to disturb, and I cannot. But what I can ask of you is that you give me time to consider, and that you in turn accept patiently the terms demanded by circumstances. Do you promise me that, Rita?"

"Yes, mamma; but Dr. Weilen?"

"He will agree to whatever you want; and this evening you yourself shall tell him. I expect him to dinner, and I asked him to come a little earlier so as to have the chance to speak to him about the birthday celebration. I shall let you report to him that he will be a welcome guest there. And then you can tell him whatever your heart dictates; but your heart must not forget that with us Jews feeling of the individual for himself must give way to feeling for something else—for the family; and that such considerations at times require personal sacrifices. These sacrifices have made us great and strong, and have aroused in us the capacity for self-surrender and self-sacrificing love. They are founded upon the noble sentiments of piety and duty. The man who loves you will understand; because very likely he unconsciously loves in you these ethical principles under which you have grown up, and which have laid their impress upon your personality, your culture, and your appearance."

Tenderly and proudly she looked at her daughter, in whom grace and modesty, dignity and humility, were charmingly blended, whose longing and love had not crowded out the feeling of obedience and compliance.

Rita kissed her mother's hand in respect and gratitude.

"And shall I not tell him that I have made you my confidante?"

"I leave that to you; only I should not like to be forced into an understanding with him now. Leave everything as it was. You were content then, and you will lose nothing by the arrangement now."

Rita withdrew. Mrs. Benas was left to her own thoughts, not free from anxiety, yet full of hope for the happiness of her daughter.

* * *

The Benases and their guests, Dr. Weilen and Dr. Rosenfeld, were spending the evening together most agreeably. The dinner had passed off pleasantly. Mr. Benas was in a happy frame of mind, and his good spirits dispelled the reserve and formality that at first prevailed. Dr. Weilen, with his usual tact and good nature, promptly fell in with and abetted the high spirits of his host. Mrs. Benas, too, after momentary embarrassment, contributed in her refined and clever manner and with her considerate hospitality, to the pleasure of the small circle. Hugo was not so brusque as usual, owing to the benignant influence of his friend Henry. Rita seemed transformed by her secret happiness. Modest and reserved as she always was, her silence was not noticed. At times she glanced at Victor's face; and when their eyes happened to meet in love and perfect understanding, the blood rose precipitately to her cheeks. They had had a talk before dinner was served, and Rita had given him the news that he was to be welcomed at Uncle Leopold's celebration. He had gathered her in his arms, and pressed a kiss upon her forehead. "My wife, my dear wife," he said with emotion. She drew closer to him, but made no answer. Such was their betrothal—not the passionate, stormy love with which he had courted her on New Year's Day, but as though devoutly consecrating her. And she was happy.

Then she told him of her conversation with her mother, and spoke of his letter, which had given her a deep insight into his life, and had brought consolation to her as well as to her mother, especially upon one point. She hesitated as she said this, and he sealed her lips with a kiss: "No, truly, I am no apostate! and my love and faith toward you will last forever, no matter what may come. And you, Rita?"

"Nothing shall separate me from you," she answered simply but resolutely, as if registering a vow.

Then they talked of her mother's request, and he readily consented to respect it. "If I am certain of your love, then I can reconcile myself to keeping this happiness to myself, until I can joyously proclaim it to the whole world. I must consent to the conditions your mother imposes, however trying they may be. At all events I shall see you; and we share a secret that makes us happy, and brings us yet closer together, if possible. When I look at you, my eyes will tell you that I love you, and I shall know that you are mine. And our eyes will meet in kisses, and every pressure of the hand will tell you of my hopes and longings. And this secret language which only we two understand will be more eloquent than spoken words."

Tears stood in her eyes. When he saw her before him, in her sweet purity and virgin modesty, it seemed impossible to him to carry out his self-denying resolutions. He drew her to him again, and said excitedly: "And must I do without you, be with you and not enfold you, not kiss you? Impossible! How long must it be?"

Then he became calm again. "Well, then, it must be."

When later on, Mrs. Benas entered, he kissed her hand. Not a word was said; yet they knew that each understood the other and that they were in accord. When the rest of the company joined them, nothing betrayed their secret conference. After dinner they gathered in the small drawing-room. Dr. Weilen's tactfulness made it easy to guide the conversation into general channels. He told of the successes of Germany's colonial policy, and what far-reaching significance it possessed.

"I do not quite understand why this policy is so obstinately opposed here," said Mr. Benas.

"It is because the masses are short-sighted, and appreciate nothing that cannot be realized in the near future. Their hand-to-mouth mode of living is the standard by which they measure everything. Why spend money upon ventures that will profit only future generations? Decidedly not. What nonsense! Here are the pennies, here is the bread for their own stomachs. What business of ours is it, if the coming generation eats cake instead of hard, dry bread? To-day's policy knows no to-morrow. Such is the logic of the narrow-minded and the illiberal, the philosophy of an insect with one day to live. It is obvious why the people espouse the policy, but it will not do to have it become the dominant policy. It has always been necessary to force upon the masses what was for their own good. Reformers and tyrants have had to apply the same formulæ. They have always had to be firm, resolute, not easily discouraged. They had to rule! Whatever they regarded as right, had to be carried through at every cost. World-power cannot be attained under a narrow local policy."

"Do you set great store by our colonial policy?"

"Decidedly so. For a long time I worked in the colonial department, and even now I take pleasure in following up our colonial affairs. The more I look into the matter, the more I am convinced that a world-power can be properly developed only upon a colonial basis."

"The Palestinian agricultural colonies for the Eastern Jews are also a part of the colonial policy," Hugo said; and addressing himself directly to Dr. Weilen, he added: "I don't know whether this has ever occupied your attention."

"Surely it has; how can you doubt it? How could anyone who is chiefly occupied with such affairs pass it by unheeding? Was it likely that I would be the exception? On the whole it is a matter that attracts more attention than is generally supposed, even in well-informed circles. The efforts now being made are well known. They are taken note of, even though not with approval. Projects for the formation of an independent government would certainly not be favored. People might smile pityingly or contemptuously at them, perhaps oppose them as hostile to the constituted authorities. But the formula of reformers and tyrants applies to the Jews as well: let them be strong of will, indomitable, not easily discouraged, and persistent."

"Dr. Weilen!" The exclamation rang with doubt and hope. Hugo stared with burning eyes, in an attempt to read Victor's meaning. Was he trifling, or was he serious? Henry likewise looked at the speaker with surprise; his eyes seemed to plead: "Do not make mock of what is sacred to us." Then a menacing expression lit up his beautiful, noble face, as he said: "The leaders of this cause are aware of the importance of their undertakings, and they surely do not lack courage to carry them through."

"Are you amongst the leaders?"

"Not yet, but I hope to be; at any rate my life is entirely dedicated to the cause."

He glanced involuntarily from Dr. Weilen to Rita, and a pained smile flitted across his lips.

Dr. Weilen caught the glance, and noticed that Rita's pale face had flushed. In a flash, he recognized the tragedy of his young life; this enthusiast loved her. But devotion to his ideals, to his unhappy race, was the stronger motive, and like a hero, he bade adieu to all desires and hopes, strangled them before they could command him. Rita must have had some suspicion of his feelings, else why had she blushed? He looked at her, but her eyes revealed only the most complete surrender to himself. Deep sympathy for Henry possessed him. A bond united them. Henry had looked on the lovely flower, had watched in silence the glorious unfolding of its petals. As a friend of her brother, her friend, too, and a favorite of the family, he might have won her. But voluntarily he renounced her, and chose to tread the thorny path, at whose distant, far distant end beckoned the fulfilment of his ideals. How could he resign her? He studied the young man. How could he give her up,—Rita? His eyes sought Rita. On her countenance lay the reflection of happy pride and inner contentment. It had made her ineffably happy to hear him speak as he did of the question that engaged her sympathies, chiefly because it formed the supreme interest of the brother to whom she was attached so intimately and lovingly. Mrs. Benas likewise showed her satisfaction with Dr. Weilen's attitude, and she looked triumphantly first at her son and then at her husband.

A slight, somewhat skeptical smile played about Mr. Benas's lips, while Hugo, not able wholly to control his excitement, exclaimed:

"And you yourself, Dr. Weilen, what is your opinion of the movement?"

"From a purely theoretical point of view, as I said, I am throughout in favor of a colonial policy. I consider the expansion and the extension of our possessions an absolute necessity in order to meet the increased needs of the nation. I admire the keen foresight of the Emperor, who has recognized this, and has made it his chief aim to fill the arteries of the kingdom with fresh, strong blood. The advantages of the undertaking will become apparent only to future generations, and it will then be difficult to understand the opposition of those who objected to his plans; and that for small considerations, because money considerations are always petty, unless they further great ends. To save at the wrong time and at the wrong place is always a poor policy; and to try to set aside important matters with trifling jests is simply stupid. You can't help despising your opponents, when you know positively that they don't understand what they oppose. In the minds of those who are thoroughly interested in the subject, there is no doubt that the coming century will be largely occupied with the development of colonial affairs, and that such measures will decidedly affect social conditions. Mistakes will be made. There will be disappointments, but every pioneer enterprise must contend with that. The method of the reformer and the tyrant will have to be enforced, as has so often been done in the history of mankind. There is a power that stands behind justice, which obstinacy converts into injustice."

Here he paused and considered. His explanations had been listened to with the greatest interest. No objection was interposed, and so he continued: "Now in regard to the colonial plans of the Jews: no objection will be made by those who have accepted the colonial policy as their programme, and who expect in the near future to see a practical fulfilment of their carefully evolved plans. Why should not the most beneficial results come from such colonization? Civilization will in its movement return from West to East, where it began. Why should not the descendants of those who carried it from its source to all quarters of the earth be the ones to bring it back? But I must not conceal from you that this is merely my personal view of the matter. Recently, when I became absorbed in the question, because I had acquired an especial interest in it,"—he said this with unmistakable pointedness—"I found that I did not look at it from a merely objective and logical point of view, but that my sentiments were involved. At crucial moments you remember that you are the great-grandson of Rabbi Akiba Friedländer. With pride I recall that our great-grandfather, Rabbi Eliezer, with one of his sons-in-law,—I think it was your father, Mrs. Benas,—was given an audience by Frederick William III in order to discuss the colonization of the Jews in Palestine, and to beg his protection. So long ago as that, and he an old Rabbi from the province of Posen! What crops out in me as a practical interest in colonial schemes, and what makes you, my friend, so deeply devoted to the cause, may be the legacy of our ancestry. Possibly this prevents us from judging these matters quite fairly; but, then, our family, in whom this idea has been kept alive for generations, may fitly uphold it without incurring the charge of being dreamers or political schemers."

He noticed how Rita's face was transfigured while he spoke. He saw that his host was pleased, and that Mrs. Benas was beaming with calm content, and showed her pleasure and pride, that a descendant of Rabbi Akiba Friedländer should hold these views. He felt Henry's inspired gaze rest upon him in questioning surprise, and in Hugo's face he read the same sentiments that filled his own soul at the time.

"If only we could shout to the entire race," the boy exclaimed, overcome with emotion, "'Don't forget your glorious past, be proud of your mission among the peoples of the earth, endure sorrow in hope of the day when you will enjoy an endless period of honor and self-confidence.'"

Rita rose involuntarily, and stood next to her brother. Henry had also drawn near to his friend; and the three young people formed an impressive group—Hugo in the proud posture of a conqueror, Henry with the devoted expression of apostolic enthusiasm, and Rita in pure happiness, the embodiment of youth and beauty awaiting victory. Dr. Weilen, regarding the trio pensively, went on to say:

"Young Israel may not be deprived of its ideals; those ideals are too worthy, too potent, to be lost; their peculiarity should be cherished, not destroyed." He looked feelingly at Rita, and she seemed to accept the glance as a promise. Mrs. Benas also read the message and a faint smile of content passed over her lips.

The conversation then assumed a more general character, although they came back several times to the subject that had given Dr. Weilen occasion to present his views. Dr. Rosenfeld found an opportunity to express his opinions of the present position of the Jews. He spoke in his melancholy, but sympathetic manner:

"It is quite inexplicable that the Jew so often lacks courage to acknowledge to himself exactly what he is. The adherents of other faiths think they must protect themselves against Jewish influence, and they fear a loss of their national peculiarities. Astounding that this instinct of self-preservation is lacking in the Jew! That he is not proud and haughty enough to defend his characteristics and to uphold them, just as the other races do, especially since his inheritance includes such worthy and brilliant qualities. Until recent times there was a bond that united the Jews, it is true, not in free, courageous self-consciousness, but in humility and subjection. The bond was their faith. But to-day, when this faith is shaken,—for as soon as the revered old forms and customs are changed, it becomes insecure,—to-day when among many Jews this faith is undermined by destructive criticism, by the onslaught of rationalism, something else must take its place, and that something is historical consciousness. Everywhere except among the Jews the feeling of nationality has reached a higher expression than ever. Yet the consciousness of their great past and of their mighty cultural development would justify their taking such a position. It is urged that the religious, conservative Israelite will continue to exist despite the modern Jew; but one thing is forgotten, that every new generation is the modern generation; the old die off to make room for the younger. But where among the new, the newer, and the newest, in generation after generation, do you find those who maintain their traditions unaltered? Let us not deceive ourselves. Where is the Jewish home to-day like the home of yesterday? The spirit of the new age has brought about a change even in families maintaining the old traditions with reverence and pride. At best, in some quiet, retired corner they build a temple in memory of the past, possibly only when an aged, venerable member of the family guards the sanctuary like a priest and patriarch."

"Rosenfeld," teased Mr. Benas, "your allusions are plainly personal."

"Forgive me, Mr. Benas," he answered, his pale face flushing, "it was no hidden allusion, but a plain reference to the example of your family, all the members of which, though living a modern life, and having discarded religious tradition, yet are preparing to celebrate a festival according to the old Jewish custom. What is bringing them together, however, is not their faith, not their customs, but one of their number, who has attained the age of a patriarch,—an old man whom they wish to honor, whom they regard with devotion and affection. This old sage will be ninety years old, and these sentiments of the occasion are purely personal, concerning a single individual. It is not faith, only filial reverence. How long will Israel continue to have patriarchs? How long will honor be brought to them? And if this bond is broken, and the historical sentiment does not grow strong in Israel to take its place, what then? There are many who say, Our mission fulfilled, we dare not complain, if we, the small minority, dissolve as an independent influence. One cannot oppose such a view; there is much to justify it, and it contains much truth. But it is a sad truth, and I should not like it to be my conviction; for I would not have my race to disappear. It is worthy to survive. It has great and glorious possibilities. Under the sunshine of a free development these will blossom forth and bear fine fruit and make Israel great among the nations."

His speech was apparently dispassionate, and his arguments were set forth clearly and objectively. But his voice vibrated, as with suppressed grief, a bitter appeal, and inner distress. His noble, quiet countenance seemed to convey a silent plaint, but the speech of his eyes was eloquent. They expressed entreaty, enthusiasm, and hope.

Mr. Benas was lost in thought, while Hugo impulsively clasped his friend's hand.

The suspense and excitement that had taken hold of all was broken only when Mrs. Benas asked them to think of more material matters, and invited them to take a glass of beer or wine and a sandwich. The clever woman had waited for the right moment. They chatted yet a while of indifferent matters. Somewhat later, when Dr. Weilen found himself alone with Rita, he asked: "Who is this Dr. Rosenfeld?"

"A student friend of Hugo's. Hugo brought him here, and he has become a favorite of all of us."

"Of you, too, Rita?"

"Yes," she said simply.

Her candor pleased him. "Have you been with him much?"

"He became my friend, especially during the last few months, when he gave me lessons in philosophy, and introduced me to the ideas of the great thinkers."

"He loves you, Rita?"

She looked at him with moist eyes, and said in a low voice: "He has never told me so."

"Who could live near you and not love you? But he is carved out of the stuff of which martyrs are made."

Involuntarily they both looked at Henry who was approaching with Hugo.

* * *

A few days before the Passover festival the excitement and bustle apt to precede great events took possession of the little town of Rawitsch. The preparations for the celebration of the ninetieth birthday of Leopold Friedländer were in full swing. Mrs. Benas and her daughter Rita had been upon the scene of action for three days. They had personally directed the preparations, and assisted their relatives. Mrs. Benas was staying with her cousin Rebecca Strelitz, the oldest daughter of Uncle Leopold. On the day after her arrival, she astonished all Rawitsch by appearing at the market with Rebecca and Friederike, the second daughter, who had married Meyer Pinkus, a city alderman. They were accompanied by the cook, whom she had sent from Berlin a week before. "The Frau Geheimrätin deigned to superintend, in her own person, the buying of turkeys and ducks and geese," the poulterer had reported at the *Minchah* service. What could not be had in the little village had been ordered from Berlin; and under the direction of Uncle Leopold's daughter-in-law Hannah, at whose house the celebration was to take place, baking and preserving and the preparing of all sorts of delicacies had been busily going on for several days, in a kitchen especially fitted out for the occasion. To Rita and to two young girls from Breslau and Mannheim,—who had also come with their mothers, the granddaughters of Uncle Leopold,—the life in the little village seemed extraordinary. The great-niece as well as the great-grandchildren had been raised under entirely different circumstances, and all the ceremonial customs observed in preparation for the week of the Passover by the entire community, but especially in the homes of their relatives, were new and strange to them. On the last evening before the beginning of the Passover they had been present at the *Chometz batteln*. The venerable old man took the lead, carrying a taper, some quills, and a large cooking spoon. He was followed by his seventy-year-old son Isidor and his wife. Thus they all went through the entire house in order to remove the last vestiges of leaven. Rita was especially impressed with the seriousness with which this was undertaken, and with the extreme significance attached to these customs. The participants clearly laid greater store by the Passover than by the anniversary celebration. The religious observance took precedence of the personal. During the day many more of the relatives arrived, among them several members of the family from the Russian city of Pinsk. They were adherents of the old Orthodoxy, with even a strong leaning in some of them toward Chassidism. They had accepted the hospitality of a distant relative who was especially pious. At the inn, "The Golden Swan," the guests from Munich and Vienna were lodged; and on the afternoon of the next day, all the rest were expected, among them Mr. Benas, Hugo, and Dr. Weilen. The tall poulterer, so-called because of his vocation of judging live poultry, was the chronicler of the village, and Shmul Weissbacher, who was called "Rebbe on the contrary," because he always took opposite sides from the person who spoke to him, ran from house to house spreading the latest news; the former circulating a rumor, the latter denying the report. The excitement in the community grew from hour to hour.

In order to make sufficient room for the table, two large chambers had been thrown into one by the removal of the partition.

The poulterer reported that they were taking out the walls of the house, while "Rebbe on the contrary" declared they weren't tearing down the walls at all, merely a bit of boarding between the rooms.

At all events Mrs. Benas's scheme furnished an appropriate apartment. The big room looked decidedly inviting, with its decorations of white bunting and green pine boughs. Adjoining was the spacious "best room" of the house; here the large doors dividing the rooms had been removed, and the tables so disposed as to form one large banquet board. The general effect was fine.

At twilight the guests assembled for the Seder. The Geheimrat, who arrived somewhat early to consult with his wife, still occupied with her arrangements, was most agreeably surprised.

"You have managed splendidly," he said, gallantly kissing his wife's hand. "Truly, wonderfully!"

Everybody agreed with him, when, after greeting the head of the family, they sat down to the table. It was covered with fine white damask, and literally glistened with silver and glass. The wine sparkled in magnificently cut caraffes. It had come with the pale oranges from the colonies of the Holy Land. Everything was arranged most effectively. The Geheimrat had kept his word, and had sent such costly, handsome silver that it might have served for the table of a prince. And like a prince Leopold Friedländer sat among his own. To-day the modest, honest, unassuming man was a king; not only the king of the family celebration, but the king of a religious festival.

In a robe of white, once his wedding costume, and later to be used as his shroud, a white cap bound with a wide silver band resting on his snow-white hair, he sat supported by soft pillows, covered with white embroidery. At his side sat his daughter-in-law, Hannah, in a grey brocade dress, with a heavy golden chain about her neck, and a cap of ivory-white lace bedecked with lilac ribbons pressed low on her forehead, the traditional head-dress of strictly orthodox Jewesses. Friederike and Rebecca, her two oldest daughters, likewise wore caps, of more modern fashion however. The relatives from Pinsk still clung to the old fashion of the silk *Sheitel*, with which a married Jewess entirely conceals her hair, replacing her natural adornment by costly jewels. Strands of pearls were wound about their heads. In fact all the Russian members of the family displayed such a wealth of diamonds and jewels that Mr. Benas could hardly suppress a smile of amusement.

The husbands of the two ladies from Pinsk were attired in long silk caftans, and side-curls escaped on each cheek from beneath their caps. In contrast to these were the elegant modern gowns worn by the rest of the family. The young women were arrayed in light airy dresses, and their coiffures—brown or blonde or reddish or deep black,—suggested Botticelli pictures. The men were in full dress.

And the company was no less diverse in its composition than in the appearance of its members. Along with the representatives of the old Judaism, which had maintained itself unchanged for centuries, all shades and grades of belief were represented. There were the orthodox, the pious, the conservative, the liberal, the reformed,—and an apostate! Similarly, all social stations were represented: high officials, an Oberverwaltungsrat, and an attorney-general from Munich—descended from the South German branch of the Friedländers—professors, physicians, lawyers, engineers, manufacturers, and merchants. There was lacking only a representative of the rabbis. There were several in the family; but they had been prevented from coming because of the necessity of officiating during the holidays. Among the younger generation there were gifted youths of studious habits, two Bavarian officers and an Austrian officer in uniform; barristers, assessors, engineers, tradesmen, and even those who had learnt a craft, and yet there was harmony in this composite picture,—a harmony created by the common sentiment possessing all in this hour.

Leopold Friedländer drew the large silver Seder platter towards him. It was decorated with the symbolic dishes of the service. The golden shells at the four corners contained the Charoseth, the bitter herbs, the egg roasted in ashes, and the salt water. In the middle were the Matzoth covered with a white silk cloth, on which were embroidered, in gold, lions supporting the shield of David worked in silver and jewels. Under this stood the blessings in Hebrew letters. A granddaughter had executed this beautiful bit of needlework. And now the treble voice of a five-year-old boy, the son of a great-great-grandchild of the patriarch, was heard saying the first words of the Haggadah: "*Mah nishtaneh ha-Layloh hazeh?*" This little boy, sitting at the table of his ancestors, was the representative of the fifth living generation. He traced his ancestry directly back to the Rabbis Eliezer and Akiba Friedländer, known as learned and high-minded men, whose virtues and piety, attainments and generosity, had brought honors to them, not only from the Jews, but also from those of other faiths. When little Jacob, in childlike tones, but clearly and distinctly asked the prescribed question, was

Leopold Friedländer thinking of his father and grandfather? For he bent over his Haggadah, and tears flowed from his weary old eyes.

Deep emotion took hold of the company. They all looked from the old man to the child,—who was staring about him with wide-open eyes and with unsuspecting curiosity,—and then again from the child to the old man. All sorts of questions and ideas crowded into the minds of the guests. The old Judaism and the new,—how would they exist together? Peacefully and quietly as in this hour? And would youth listen devoutly when age taught the lessons from the history of the race? Would the young people of the future gather about the patriarchs? Would they leave the busy life, the gay bustle of existence, its struggles, and its duties in search of consecration and peace? Such a miracle was happening in this simple Jewish home. In a spirit of reverence they followed the recital of the Haggadah, as the patriarch intoned in a feeble but impressive voice, the queer, outlandish, Talmudic, and casuistic interpretations of the festival. And when, with trembling hands, he filled the tall silver beaker with the wine destined for the prophet Elijah, he rose in his chair, and with the expression of religious faith imprinted upon his aged features, exclaimed, *Leshonoh habooh bi-Yerusholoyim,* a spirit of awe descended upon the company. No one seemed able for the moment to throw off the inspiring impression, not even those who failed to share the hopes expressed in the prayer.

Hugo Benas was most deeply affected. "So it must be," he whispered to his mother, who sat next to him. "Though worlds apart in their views, in standards of life, in position, in culture, they are united by ties of race. And wherever Jews live in this way, a spiritual Zion will arise, as here, in this humble abode."

* * *

The assembled relatives had drawn close together during these holidays. Points of contact had appeared, the old bonds had been renewed, new ones had been formed; and with complacency they told one another of the many members of the family who had attained high positions in civil life. Honor was paid to those who had kept the religious traditions uncontaminated. Undisturbed harmony reigned, and not even Victor Weilen formed a discordant element. Curiously enough, one of the Pinsker kin, who knew nothing of Victor's apostasy (for the subject had not been referred to), was most attracted to him; and Victor questioned the pious and intelligent man about the condition of the Jews in Russia. It was of interest to him to hear how the old orthodoxy had been preserved there, and had become a factor in politics, in which, despite their religious segregation, the Jews were necessarily involved. Mr. Benas, however, could not resist a good-humored yet slightly satirical remark, when he repeatedly saw these two men together. "Under the shelter of the Patriarch, the orthodox and the apostate come together," he said to Hugo, who responded: "That is Zion."

With these impressions fresh in mind, the Benases returned home; and as a result of their influence the union of Weilen with Rita was not opposed, not even by Hugo. Since the evening on which Dr. Weilen had so freely stated his views concerning colonization, Hugo had been less distant toward him, and in the course of time the relation between them grew in cordiality. They had discussed the Jewish question repeatedly, and Hugo was always agreeably impressed by the man's calm, his lack of prejudice, and his sincerity. Such qualities counted doubly in his case. They had also touched upon his change of belief, and Dr. Weilen had said in regard to it: "The new belief that I adopted could give me nothing, just as the loss of the other had taken nothing from me, because I was not devout in this sense; and that liberated me, and it keeps me free even to-day, as a mature man, to acknowledge and associate myself with those to whom I am attached by a bond which has a deeper hold than this or that rite or ceremony can possibly have."

And when Hugo saw him so full of tact, taking a cordial interest in all who flocked about the patriarch, on the spot that since then he called "Zion," he had taken him into his young heart, readily fired with enthusiasm. He understood his sister's love for this man, and he no longer resisted the inevitable outcome: that she should become his wife according to the laws of the land in which they lived. But then ... then!

The engagement was celebrated privately. On the evening of its announcement, when the family was gathered together, the Geheimrat, who had feared Hugo's impetuous disposition, and who now saw him consent so joyously, gave him a great surprise, too. This day on which his daughter was to be made so happy, should also be of special significance to his son. He announced to Hugo that he was ready to interest himself in the colonies in Palestine, and to help them financially. With overflowing gratefulness Hugo flung his arms about his father, and kissed and fondled his mother. Rita and Victor declared that they regarded this decision as their finest betrothal gift.

Hugo was happy. "Then I may dedicate myself entirely to these aims? When I have passed my final examinations?" he said, half in question and half in decision.

Mr. Benas frowned slightly: "That means I must give not only my millions but also my son to the cause?" The words sounded good-humored, yet as though he were making fun of himself. "That is building Utopia at heavy expense to me."

"Zion, father, Zion, wherever it may be."

"*Noblesse oblige*," Mrs. Benas interrupted. "That was the lesson of our visit to Uncle Leopold's, those memorable days under the shelter of the Patriarch."

"Mamma is right," said Victor. "And if all Jews thought and acted as you have done, dear father, then happiness and hope would find lodging even among the unfortunate members of our persecuted race, and blessings would spring up. Where? Well, the world is so big and so great.... Civilization is so eager to conquer, and Israel so persistent and enduring."

His tone was cordial, convincing, and soothing.

Involuntarily Rita stepped to his side, and he drew her gently to him.

"And he who speaks thus, father, is—"

"He is the *fiancé* of our daughter, of your sister, Hugo," Mr. Benas quickly interrupted.

*　*　*

It was spring time. In beauty and splendor the spring had taken possession of the earth! In youth, joy, and glory everything seemed changed, and awakened to new life by the sweet kisses of the sun. Lovers are peculiarly sensitive to such joy. Entranced, Rita and Victor were looking out from the terrace of the house upon the park, which, in its green attire, lay before them in Easter splendor. Victor had taken Rita's hand, and held it in silent happiness.

Hugo approached them with two open letters in his hand.

"Mother said I should find you here."

"Is it not beautiful here, Hugo?" asked his sister. "At this time of the year Berlin always seems wonderful to me, especially out here. How glorious it is!"

He paid no attention to her remarks and said: "I looked for you to show you these letters, one from Henry, and the other...." He looked at one of the letters. "Elkish informs me that he has decided to retire."

Her expression became sad: "We might have foreseen that," she said in a low voice.

"He wishes to return with his sister to his home in Lissa."

"What does father say?"

"He feels he must accept the resignation, and will, of course, allow him a proper pension."

Victor had listened in silence to the conversation between sister and brother.

"Is he an old retainer of your house?"

Rita nodded assent.

"Is he going because I have come? Does his fanaticism drive him away?"

"Perhaps, but may be he is worn out."

It was apparent from the tone of her voice that she herself had no faith in her reassuring words.

"O no," said Hugo, "he goes because he can no longer comprehend us, so he writes, and he does not wish to make the leave-taking hard, therefore...."

"He does not wish to see me again?" Rita cried out in pain.

Superiority was sharply expressed in his countenance, strong self-consciousness, untempered by sympathy. Rita looked at Weilen as though to beg his pardon, while Hugo's serious eyes gazed into vacancy. For several minutes there was silence, then Dr. Weilen asked: "And what does your friend Rosenfeld write?"

Hugo breathed freely, as if a burden had been lifted from off his soul. "He! He wishes you joy from the bottom of his heart. He is delighted to hear that Rita is happy." Then he looked over the letter as if searching for a particular passage. "Here: 'I thank you for the news of your sister's engagement. Such a girl's choice can only bring happiness, and make her happy; for truth and purity are united in her, and such natures as hers are sure to find what is right. What little I know of Dr. Weilen warrants this assurance. Dr. Weilen seems to me a man of deep insight and fine feeling, in whom strength and tenderness go together—qualities desirable in the husband of a highly intellectual woman like Rita. Devout in her tender soul and tolerant in her clear head, that is her personality. Her mission is to minister to the happiness of one individual. But as for us, we must think of the common weal, and to it we will dedicate our strength and our blood. And now let us set forth on the road, even though it be wearisome. Let us be up and doing.... Let us labor in behalf of our co-religionists." He folded the letter. "Yes, that shall be our mission."

Mr. and Mrs. Benas had stepped into the door and stood looking at their children. They had overheard Hugo's last words, and they appreciated the solemnity of the moment. And the consummation of their hopes was glorified by the soft, golden radiance of the spring.

GLOSSARY

(All words given below, unless otherwise specified, are Hebrew. The transliteration aims to reproduce the colloquial pronunciation of Hebrew words by German Jews.)

AL CHET. "For the sin," beginning of a confession of sins.

AMHOREZ. Ignoramus.

AMRAZIM. Plural of the previous word. Ignoramuses.

BAAL-MILCHOMOH. Soldier.

BAALE-BATIM. Householders. Substantial and respectable members of the community, who contribute to its support.

BAR-MITZVAH. Religious majority, at the age of thirteen, when a Jewish lad is expected to take all religious duties upon himself.

BEKOVET. Honorable; dignified.

BESOMIM. Spices, used at the ceremony of *Habdalah*, marking the end of the Sabbath.

BORUCH HA-SHEM. "Blessed be the Name" (of God).

CHAROSETH. A mixture of apples, raisins, wine, cinnamon, etc., used at the *Seder*, symbolic of the mortar which the Israelites prepared in Egypt.

CHAS VE-SHOLEM. "Mercy and peace." Heaven forbid!

CHAVRUSSEH. Society; company.

CHAZEN. Cantor; precentor.

CHOCHMES. Wise ideas; oversubtle notions.

CHOMETZ BATTELN. To do away with all leaven (before Passover).

CHUTZPEH. Arrogance; audacity; impudence.

DAVVENING (?). Reciting the prayers of the liturgy.

EVADDE. Assuredly; certainly.

FROMM (Ger.). Pious; observant (of religions and ritual ceremonies).

GEMOREH. The Talmud.

GET. A bill of divorce.

GOY. A non-Jew.

KHILLE. Jewish congregation; Jewish community.

KIDDUSH. Sanctification; the ceremony ushering in the Sabbath or a holiday.

KOSHER. Ritually permitted.

MAASEH. A story; an anecdote.

MAH NISHTANEH HA-LAYLOH HAZEH. "What distinguishes this night" (from all other nights); the question introducing the narrative of the Exodus from Egypt in the Seder service of the Passover nights.

MAIREV. Evening service.

MALKEH. Queen.

MATZOTH. Cakes of unleavened bread.

MELECH. King.

MENORAH. Candlestick used on *Chanukkah* or Sabbath.

MESHUGGE. Crazy.

MESHUMMED. Apostate.

MIKVEH. Ritual bath.

MINCHAH. Afternoon service.

MINYAN. A company of ten men, the minimum for a public service.

MISHPOCHEH. Family in the wider sense; collateral branches as well as direct descendants; kin.

MOGEN DOVID. "The Shield of David." A Jewish emblem.

NARRONIM. (Ger. with Heb. ending). Fools.

NEBBICH. (Slavic). An expression of pity. Poor thing! Too bad!

OMED. Reading desk of the cantor in the synagogue.

OSER. "Forbidden." Expression of defiance: You bet I won't; I'd like to catch myself, etc.

OSHAMNU BOGADNU. "We have trespassed, we have dealt deceitfully." First two words in the alphabetic confession of sins.

OVINU MALKENU. "Our Father, our King." Beginning of the lines of a well-known prayer. *See next word.*

OVINU MALKENU CHOSVENU BE-SEFER PARNOSSOH VE-CHALKOLOH. "Our Father, our King, inscribe us in the book of sustenance and maintenance." One line of a well-known prayer.

PARCHONIM. Riff-raff; small fry; vermin.

PESACH. Feast of Unleavened Bread; Passover.

PLEITEGEHER. (Heb. and Ger.). An habitual bankrupt.

POSHEH YISROEL. "A sinner in Israel"; one who disregards the ceremonial law of Judaism.

RAV. Officiating rabbi.

REBBETZIN. (Heb. with Ger. suffix). Wife of the officiating rabbi.

ROSHEKOL. Head of the Jewish community.

SEDER. Home service on the first two nights of the Passover.

SHABBES. Sabbath.

SHABBES GOY. A non-Jew engaged, often by all the families in a Jewish congregation, to do work forbidden the Jew on the Sabbath, such as kindling a fire, etc.

SHADCHEN. Marriage broker.

SHAMMES. Verger; beadle; sexton.

SHEITEL (Ger.). A covering for the head, to hide the hair of a married Jewess.

SHEM YISBORACH. "The Name (of God) be blessed."

SHEMA YISROEL. "Hear, O Israel"; beginning of the Jewish confession of faith.

SHICKSEL. (Heb. with Ger. suffix). Drastic expression for a non-Jewish girl.

SHIKKER. Habitual drunkard.

SHIVEH. "Seven" days of mourning, immediately after a death occurs in a family.

SHIVOH OSER BE-TAMUZ. "Seventeenth Day of Tamuz"; a fast day commemorating the first breach in the walls of Jerusalem by Nebuchadnezzar, who took the Temple itself three weeks later.

SHNORRERS (Ger.). Beggars.

SHOLOSH SUDES. The third meal on the Sabbath.

SHUL (Ger.). Synagogue.

SHULCHAN ORUCH. The Jewish code of ritual laws, etc.

SUKKOTH. Feast of Tabernacles.

TALLES. Prayer-scarf.

TALMID CHOCHOM. A Jewish scholar, learned specifically in Jewish lore.

TASHLICH. "Thou wilt cast"; ceremony connected with the afternoon of the first day of New Year, and observed at a running stream or at the seashore.

TREFA. Ritually unfit for food.

TZORES. Trials; tribulations.

WAIGESCHRIEEN (Ger.). Woe is me.

YEVORECHECHO ADONAY VE-YISHMERECHO. "May the Lord bless thee and keep thee."

YICHUS. Aristocracy; good family connections.

YIDDISHKEIT (Ger.). Jewishness.

YOM KIPPUR. Day of Atonement.

YONTEF. Holiday; festival.

ZECHER ZADDIK LIVROCHOH. "The remembrance of the righteous is for a blessing."

ZECHUS. Merit; privilege.

ZICHRONO LIVROCHOH. "His memory is for a blessing."

Milton Keynes UK
Ingram Content Group UK Ltd.
UKHW010627080324
438959UK00005B/337